SING ME a Song

A. Rone

Copyright

Trigger Warning

This novella contains incredibly detailed and very explicit scenes of sexual assault, rape, torture, and murder. Scenes of gore and extreme violence. If you are triggered in any way by these, please do not read any further.

"Through music you hypnotize people and when you get them at their weakest point you can preach into their subconscious what we want to say."

– Jimi Hendrix

RAIDEN

C.A. RENE

Prologue

1983 – Loving Beginnings Orphanage

"Say your bedtime prayers, boys." Sister Jane says from the doorway of our room. "Father Robert will be here shortly to bless you."

"No!" I hear my brother whisper and begin to cry.

Father Robert is not a nice man and he's been blessing us twice a week for three years now. His blessings don't feel nice and he likes to pick one of us to receive it while the others watch.

I wish my parents never left me or my brother because we went from a bad place to another way worse. This feels like the Hell the sisters are always teaching us about. It's filled with demons and the devil who watches us, then wants us to burn forever with him.

Father Robert seems more like the devil and the sisters are demons, they all feel evil. What did I do wrong? Why was I sent to Hell before I died? Is it because my parents were bad people?

The light turns out and I can hear a few of the boys begin to cry along with my baby brother. I want to help them but I'm just as weak and afraid.

We hear the footsteps thudding in the hall, coming for our room, and I listen as the boys all begin to hush. He tends to pick the one most upset.

The door creaks open, I see his outline from the hallway light, and bury my face under the covers.

"Hello, children of God." His deep voice circles around our heads. "Who wants to be blessed?"

We all remain silent and I pray he changes his mind, or the Devil comes to take him away to burn forever.

"Victor." My heart stops and I hear my brother's wail. "Come see your father, child."

I hear a struggle and then a loud slap as I imagine Father Robert's hand connecting with my little brother's face.

I throw back my covers and stand on my bed just in time to see Father Robert forcing Victor to slip under his robes.

"No!" I shout and Father Robert looks at me. "I want to do it tonight."

His smile scares me and his yellow teeth stand out against his thin pink lips.

"Raiden." He claps once. "I'm happy to see you are becoming eager for your blessings."

He shoves Victor out and he lands on his bum on the hard floor. He whimpers and begins to crawl back to his bed. I am his big brother and Mommy made me promise to always protect him. I can't break my promise.

"Come now."

I get off the bed and drag my feet forward, if I do it just how he likes, it'll be over quickly. He lifts his robes when I'm standing in front of him and I see his privates, hairy and strange. I shuffle forward and his hand lands on top of my head.

"Watch now, children." His voice begins to sound weird. "Watch how Raiden collects his blessing."

1995 – Enlightened Records

"We've saved you from the clutches of evil," Magistra Karen tells us from behind her large desk, "now we need a few things from you."

"Don't you want to be famous?" Magister Camden asks.

"Yes." The four of us answer in unison.

"Don't you want to be rich?" Magister Markus asks.

"Yes." We repeat.

"The elders believe you are destined for greatness and want to help you with every one of your desires. All they require is sacrifices." Magistra Karen smiles, her teeth much like Father Robert's.

"We want to bring you into the fold here in New York and especially into our Parish. We are appointing you a manager. His name is Magus Kenny." Magister Camden says.

A guy about our age steps out of the shadows of the room and nods in our direction.

"What sacrifices?" Torrent asks. My little brother does not like the thought of serving others.

"Souls." Magistra Karen replies. "Many souls."

Chapter One

My fingertips skim down between my breasts and slowly glide over my taut stomach. The heavy beat of The Take by Tory Lanez and Chris Brown washes over me as the heat from the fluorescents above heats my skin. I'm restless and craving the release only my body can provide. The beat quickens so I reach for the pole above my head and pivot until I'm face to face with it. The cool steel warms against my palms as I lift myself up and wrap my legs around it tightly.

The room sways and the fog thickens. I release my hands, letting my legs hold me in place. I lean back until I am parallel with the pole, my back hitting the cool metal, my vision upside down, as I stare out into the blurry faces of hungry looking men.

My heartbeat kicks up, I grab my tits in my hands, and give them a rough squeeze. That does it, the men stand in a frenzy and throw their wads of bills onto the stage.

Predictable assholes.

I rotate around the pole slowly until my hands touch the floor and then I hold myself in a handstand, letting my legs fall apart into a split. I let my body slowly fall over and land on the floor, stretching my arms over my head. I twerk my ass for good measure then look over my shoulder to the crowd of men vying for my attention.

The lights go dark and I pull myself back up to standing.

"That was Tempest. Who wants to see more of her?" The crowd goes wild at the MC's words and I saunter backstage. "She's here every night, same time."

Every night. How fucking sad does that sound? It's fucking pathetic really that I come here because I have nothing at home. I snort at that thought, home, I live in a one room apartment because living in New York is fucking expensive. It's even more expensive when you must pay off a mountain of debt your cancer ridden father leaves with his death.

Aw fuck, I slap the wall as I walk towards the dressing room. I'm starting to feel shit again and that can't happen, I don't have time to feel shit.

I round the corner into the room and see Sky sitting on her vanity, her feet on the edge, and her knees spread wide. Chanel has her head buried so deep between them, I almost worry she may be suffocating.

"Good night?" Sky asks, her question ending on a moan. I hear Chanel slurping and roll my eyes.

"Probably." I shrug and sit at my vanity. I pull out the vial in my top drawer and dump some of the white powder onto the glass top.

I cut out my lines with a credit card that's completely maxed and lean over, snorting the first line deep into my left nostril. None of us have a stitch of clothing on because what's the fucking point? It all comes off anyways and besides none of us are ashamed of what we have.

"Fuck yes." Sky moans and I look over my shoulder as she rides Chanel's face. "I'm coming."

Chanel's hand goes between her own legs as she works her clit and gets Sky off at the same time. Sky's head tips back with a moan and Chanel begins to tremble between her legs, both girls coming at the same time and neither are lesbians. How fucking poetic.

Chanel stands up and brushes her bushy blonde hair off her shoulders. She's tall, standing at six feet and rail thin, I can count every one of her ribs, well the ones not obstructed by the biggest pair of fake tits.

"Tempest," Chanel bends over me to fix her smudged mascara. "Can I borrow your gold G-String?"

"You can have it if you're borrowing it." I snap and bend over to sniff the next line into my right nostril.

The burn is fast but the tingles that spread over my head feels amazing and the sudden feeling of weight lifting off my shoulders is more addicting than the shit itself.

"Sounds like you need a good pussy eating, too." Sky snorts behind me as she lights a joint.

Sky is the type of gorgeous that's loud and in your face. Her features can take your breath away and her body can elicit immediate arousal. She used to do it to me constantly when I first started working here three months ago.

She's tall with a pair of never-ending legs, she has long box braids that end at her tailbone and her eyes pop out of her face like golden orbs. Her skin is like a rich smooth umber and those lips are what I use as reference when I get my own plumped. There's no one else that walks that stage as beautiful as Sky.

Sky, Chanel, Diamond, Goldie, Queen, and I are just some of the regular girls that twerk our asses on the regular here at The Temple. They all use stage names to sensationalize their stage persona and I say they because mine is not.

Tempest Skeigh Verona is my real name and when Carl read that, I was hired on the spot. Didn't matter that I was once a dance prospect for Juilliard or that I had already worked as a burlesque dancer in Vegas. The name is what got me hired.

That's what happens when you have a crackhead mother hell bent on naming you something no other kid in the trailer park would have. She succeeded.

"I need a man between my legs," I grin at her. "Not into seeing a fried box dyed head."

"Hey!" Chanel hollers from across the room. "Shut the fuck up, bitch!"

"Yeah," Sky snickers. "Not everyone can wear no makeup and still look like Megan Fox on her best day."

Whatever. I roll my eyes. Megan Fox. Maybe a doped-up stripper who hasn't slept in days and needs a proper meal, version of Megan Fox. It's the jet-black hair, grey/green eyes, and a pouty lip combo. The tall and lean-I live off ramen and coffee-look. My rump is my best asset and my tits are small, I'm just too nervous to go under the knife or else they'd be fucking beach balls.

Doesn't matter though, my tits may be apples but I am still the highest paid dancer here. Thanks to me, according to Carl, traffic has increased by fifty percent since I showed up wet and exhausted looking for a job. And that's just stage work because you will never see me going to the back for private shows. I won't be sucking or fucking any dick that comes through those doors, I may be a drug addicted stripper with barely any money to my name, but I still have my fucking pride.

"Temp, Sky." Carl appears at the door. "Can you

stay later tomorrow night? I have a meeting and I need a few girls on the poles."

These late-night meetings usually bring me the fattest tips because Carl entertains the high-end drug dealers and seedy looking men dressed in top-of-the-line tailored suits. He usually pairs me up with Sky and if we touch each other a bit or make out, it really ramps up those Benjamin's.

"Sure." Sky calls out and I toss him a nod.

"Thanks, ladies." He scratches at his chin and looks slightly nervous. "It's for Raiden's celebration."

I raise a brow not knowing what he's talking about and swing my head to Sky when I hear her gasp.

"Carl," she begins to shake her head.

"It's just the meeting. Not the choosing." He tries to convince her.

"Who are they?" I ask him.

"They are the devil incarnate." Sky mutters and gnaws on her lip.

"I'll do it alone." I tell Carl. "Don't force her if she doesn't want to."

"No, Temp." Sky rushes over to me. "You can't do it either."

"I need the money, Sky." I shake my head at her.

"Okay, Tempest." Carl nods. "You're my best. I think you up there alone will be enough."

I watch as he leaves the doorway and his footsteps echo down the hall.

"Listen, Temp." Sky lays her hand on my shoulder. "Whatever you do, don't make eye contact and do not talk to any of them. Shake your ass and then leave as soon as the meeting is done."

"Sky, what the fuck?" I stare at her with wide

eyes. "Why are you so scared of these men?"

We see scary looking sons of bitches in here all the time, this shit isn't new, so I can't figure out what the fuck her issue is.

"Just do as I say." She says as the MC calls her name to the stage. She gives me a pointed look and repeats, "just do as I say."

SING ME a Song

Chapter Two

"I fucking bagged a thousand last night." I say as I cut the lines out on my vanity.

"Plus, you're doing overtime tonight, so shit girl, you're rolling in it." Queen purrs in her raspy voice and her dark eyes glow with envy.

Queen is exactly what her name is, she's the longest running stripper here, and hitting almost forty. She looks good for her age and that's why Carl keeps her on but her attitude is shit. She's short but she has all the right curves and a cute little pixie haircut on her platinum hair.

"Mmhmm." I nod then sniff a line.

Not one person who works in this hole in the ground is sober. We all have a vice and Queen's is the little travel sized vodka bottles you'd find in a cheap motel's bar fridge. She downs about five in a row before she hits the stage and then another three when she gets off. I don't judge, I get it, I need this shit to help me walk out there, too.

I was supposed to become a famous dancer, travel the world, marry prestigious, and raise little brats. Things change in a heartbeat with the entertainment business and you can go from slurping caviar to ramen noodles in an instant.

"I wonder if Carl will be having his annual meeting tonight." Queen hums. "Those men really are delectable."

"You've worked one of these meetings?" I ask, finally finding someone who will tell me something. "What has Sky so afraid of them?"

"Sky's a little pussy." Queen sneers and I roll my eyes. "If I still had a little pussy, I'd be out there tonight, too." Gross.

"There must be a reason she doesn't want to be there." I press and Queen chugs back one of her mini bottles.

"They sometimes hire the girls for private shows and some of them never come back."

"Like they go missing?" I gasp.

"No girl, I would assume they pay them well enough that they don't need to come back. One stint lasted three days and five girls were paid fifteen g's each. One of them didn't come back, she wasn't here long anyways. You should ask Tiny, she was there."

Tiny, she's our plus sized stripper and let me tell you, she can work a pole better than most here.

"Tiny went?" I question.

"Yeah, one of the guys has a thing for big girls." She shrugs.

Tiny is back on shift tomorrow, I won't be able to question her tonight before the meeting but I'll be able to rest my curiosity about the whole thing tomorrow.

"Temp!" Freight calls out from the corridor. "You're up."

Freight is our security and lives up to the name we've given him. He's as big as a Mack truck and will run anyone down that tries to harm us. He's the reason I feel safe staying here late because he walks each of us to our cars at night.

I stand and readjust my black bikini top and turn to study my assless chaps. I'm wearing the smallest G-string known to fucking man because we can't get completely naked in New York, but you can be damn sure pussy lip slips are a thing. I grab my cowgirl hat on the way out and wink at Freight.

"Save a horse, ride a cowgirl?" I ask him.

His mouth twitches with the beginning of a grin and I chuckle. It's the most I've ever gotten him to smile.

Big & Rich's Save a Horse starts playing on the sound system and Mouth-our MC-growls into the mic.

"It's that time again, folks." He croons. "She's oiled, she's primed, and you best believe she's going to be leaving this stage wet."

"Ew," I mutter. "Can he be any skeevier?"

"Yeah, he can." Freight nods, his voice deep.

The lights drop low and fog begins to rise from under the stage, slowly rolling over it.

"Tempest Skeigh." Mouth moans over the mic and I gag.

I part the curtain and slowly strut out on stage, my hat low covering my upper face. I walk right up to the edge and see feet below me, looks like I've brought in enough to occupy the front row. I slowly rotate my hips back, running my hand down my torso and over my mound. Then the music picks up and I grab my pussy, gyrating into my hand as I throw my hat out to the crowd. One of the bar hop girls will grab it for me later.

My jet-black hair tumbles in waves down my back as I swing around and drop to my knees. I let my legs slowly slide apart, giving them a full show of my ass and pussy, then leisurely crawl towards the pole. A few men call out and some whistle as I reach up for the pole, dragging myself to standing.

I twirl around it once and then stop, the pole at my back and my back to the crowd. I arch and press my ass against the steel, letting the pole glide between my ass cheeks. The cool metal meets the sensitive skin between my cheeks as I gradually drop forward and twerk my ass against the pole.

The crowd erupts with hoots and hollers, as the paper bills hit the stage. It doesn't take much to gain a man's attention, the work comes with trying to keep it, and that is what's made me so damn popular.

I turn around and shoot the crowd a wink as I rotate my wrist above my head, like I'm readying a lasso. I run my other hand back down my torso and flick open the button on the front.

"Please fuck me, beautiful." An older man pants at the front of the stage.

Not a cold chance in Hell, I throw him a wink anyways, and grin when I see him toss a couple hundred-dollar bills on the stage.

I bend over as I push my chaps down my legs, giving the crowd an ample look at my perky tits, and stand up to step out of them. Then I hold my hands up towards the ceiling and rotate my hips seductively, like I'm riding a cock.

I feel my barely there scrap of material wedge up and between my pussy lips. I squat down, opening my legs wide, and begin to hump forward. By now, the men have basically seen my pussy, all except that glistening hole, and that's what has them focused. They want to catch a glimpse and they refuse to look away in case they miss it.

I come back up, moving my body in a seductive

wave as I untie the strings on the back of my bikini top. I pull it off, dropping it to the stage, and grip my tits in my hands.

I don't know why, it's just a feeling of being pulled, like I have lost control of my eyes, and suddenly I am looking out past the crowd towards the back booths where four men sit. They don't look like our usual patrons, they aren't wearing suits, no leather cuts, and certainly not a badge. No, these men are dressed in oversized hoodies, the hoods obscuring half their faces, and dark wash jeans.

I finish my dance and slowly turn, my eyes staying on those four until my back is facing them, and I walk behind the curtain.

Who the fuck were they? Two of them had long graying beards, like old men, not that that's weird around here, just that they were giving off younger vibes with their attires.

"Tempest Skeigh." Mouth moans into the mic. "She won't give you a lap dance but she'll touch that pretty pussy for you."

Fucking gross.

"They're here." An arm shoots out of an open door and pulls me into a darkened room.

"Sky?" It's her voice, I just don't know why she's acting like a weird moron. "Aren't you off tonight?"

"Girl, they saw you. They have their eyes set on you." She sounds petrified. "You're going to be chosen."

"Okay, I need you to take several deep breaths and tell me what the fuck is going on."

"I know you saw them, everyone notices them when they come in here." She's whispering and the grip she has on my arm is lethal.

"Girl, I need to put some clothes on. It's cold and

you're clearly high as fuck." I try to yank my arm out of her grasp.

"Listen, Temp." She hauls me in closer. "Don't do this tonight. Just go home right now, these guys are fucking weird, and I've heard strange stories."

"Like what?"

"It's a long story. Leave with me right now and I'll tell you everything." Her nails leave behind red indents in my skin.

"I spoke to Queen and she said it's no big deal." I finally unwedge myself from her grip. "Tiny went to one of their events. I don't know what's wrong with you!"

"I warned you, it's all I can do." She says and leaves the room.

I finally see her in the dim light of the corridor, she's dressed in oversized clothing, and looks unrecognizable.

The apprehension that skates down my spine has my hair on end and my heart skipping a beat.

Sing Me a Song

Sacrificial Lambs

TEMPEST

C.A. RENE

Chapter Three

The floor length mink coat Carl gave me is tickling my nose and the fact that I'm wearing nothing underneath has me slightly unnerved. I know this is after hours and I know all the same rules don't apply but I thought pussy was completely off limits.

Carl assured me they wouldn't touch but that they like certain things, and one of those things is a bare pussy. Whatever, I don't care I'll be leaving here with a couple grand in my pocket and that's all that matters. Let the fuckers look.

"Tempest, any particular song you want?" Mouth asks from behind me.

"I really don't care." I shrug. I really don't. I just snorted enough coke to down a bear, I'm good.

He stares at me until I raise a brow and then he's scooting back to his booth.

"Ready?" Freight asks.

"Yeah." I nod. The movement makes my head spin and vision blur.

Freight pulls back the black curtain and I ascend the three steps to the stage. The room is dimmer than usual and the place feels more intimate as the music plays softly in the background. I saunter to the pole and look out across the room. The place is empty save for a table in the back occupied by those four guys I saw earlier, Carl, and a fifth I haven't seen before.

I let the feel of the music move my body and I let go of any thoughts lingering in my mind. I don't care about that table and the men occupying it. Right now, I care only to enjoy this high and have this next hour pass me by.

I last about fifteen minutes in that fur atrocity and then I shrug it off, throwing it aside. It's hot in here and I can't be bothered if I'm as naked as the day I was born.

The men are preoccupied with their conversation because not one of them has noticed me and if they have, they've been discreet about it. Carl looks a bit stressed as he gnaws on his lip and drags his fingers across his forehead, making me more curious as to what is being said.

The original four men are still mostly covered by their hoods and baggy clothing but the fifth member to join them looks professional in a three-piece suit and what looks to be an expensive silk tie. He screams overwhelming wealth and even though his face looks older, he still has smoldering handsome features.

I've seen men like him visit the trailer park whores or drug dealers and assume we all look up to them for how well they're dressed, little do they know that we're watching to see when we can steal their wallets.

They all rise from their seats simultaneously and I realize I haven't moved in the past five minutes. Fuck it, I'm high as a motherfucker. I slowly gyrate my hips as I try to look like I haven't been intensely watching them. Carl is sweating as he nods profusely at the suited fucker that's waving his pointer finger at him, and the other four have their arms crossed identically over their wide chests.

Suit cunt slaps his hand into Carl's arm and the five of them file out towards the exit with the suit in the lead.

No one looks my way, even though I'm up here without a stitch on and I can't help but watch as they slowly walk by. It's the last guy-the biggest of the bunch-that turns his head and his tattoo covered hand comes out of his hoodie pocket as he flicks something towards me. I blame my current high for my slow reaction because I look to my feet and see a black switchblade embedded into the stage less than an inch from my big toe.

"Are you fucking serious?" I call out as their backs disappear through the exit.

None of them turn to look at me or the commotion I'm causing on the stage, they just open the doors and disappear into the night.

Freight runs up on the stage cursing and throws the fur jacket over my shoulders. Then he bends and pulls the blade out of the wood. The handle and blade are both black save for an insignia etched into the handle. I try to see what it is when I hear Carl muttering from the floor and turn to look at him.

He's pale and his eyes are wide as he stares at the knife in Freight's hand. "Take her back."

"Why the fuck did they do that?" I ask him, my heart beating wildly. He almost took off my fucking toe.

Carl just shakes his head and continues to stare at the fucking knife. What the fuck just happened? I feel Freight's arm wrap around my shoulders and he steers me back through the curtain.

"Give me that knife." I hold out my hand.

"Are you su..."

"Give me the fucking knife." I cut him off and he places it in my hand.

I storm off for the dressing room and throw the fur jacket into a dusty corner. I sit at my vanity and flip the knife over in my hands. The whole thing feels like a carbide material, lightweight and smooth, but the blade itself is gleaming with a sharpened edge. Was he aiming for my fucking foot? Did he want the blade to sink through my flesh? I shiver at the thought and hold the handle closer to my face.

There is an etching on either side, one side has what looks to be a weird, shaped lightning bolt, and the other has the name Raiden. Raiden? Is that his name? The fucker that tried to disfigure me and for no fucking reason.

"Raiden James." Carl's voice floats in from the doorway. "He's the lead singer of the band Deluge."

I don't have a single clue who the fuck Deluge is but the name Raiden is sounding familiar. I twist the knife in my hands and read the name again. Raiden.

"They come once a year to procure a few girls to work Raiden's birthday." It's like he can read my thoughts.

"Why would an old dude throw a knife at me?" I ask him.

"You were chosen."

SING ME a Song

Sacrificial Lambs

TEMPEST

C.A. RENE

Chapter Four

I was chosen, simple right?

I've been moping around my one room apartment all day, this knife still firmly in my grasp, and a wine bottle to my face. Carl told me to take the next few days off to recoup but what the fuck am I recouping from? Almost losing a digit? Besides, he and I both know I can't take a few days off. I have rent due and about eight credit cards that I have to pay the minimum balance on.

I chug back the bit of wine left in the bottom of the bottle and grab my purse, dropping the knife inside. Might as well shake my ass and make a few dollars for it.

My car pulls into the lot and the brakes squeal as I come to a halt. Fuck off, how much more shit can go wrong? I get out of the car and slam the door with anger. I hear something rattle when I do and cringe at what I can only imagine will cost a fortune. I storm inside and see Chanel sitting at the bar, flirting with Kyle. He's our hot bartender and every girl here has tried to sleep with him, except me.

Don't get me wrong, he's fucking gorgeous, built, and covered in tattoos, I just haven't wanted anything to do with dick in a long time. Or pussy for that matter. I've had my head stuck in my finances and had no time to fucking think of anything else.

"Tempest!" Chanel calls out as she hurries to follow me into the back. "Everyone is talking about you today."

"Is that right?" I ask over my shoulder.

"Is it true? Did Raiden choose you?"

I stop abruptly and turn to face Chanel just as she stops herself from crashing into me.

"What the fuck does that mean?" I growl into her face. Everyone wants to fucking talk but not one person can give me an answer.

"It means he wants you at his party, you don't have to go through the choosing." She shrugs.

"What the actual fuck is a choosing?"

"They have certain tastes. One likes the big girls, another likes the more ethnic. Stuff like that."

"All for a fucking birthday party?" I throw my hands up.

"It's Deluge, they were a huge rock band in the nineties." Chanel's brow lifts at my ignorance.

"Never heard of them." I couldn't afford a fucking CD player or whatever it is these old fuckers released their music on. And my parents weren't huge into music, mostly just drugs and alcohol.

"Look them up! Some of their shit is dark but so good."

"I'll pass." Considering one of them tried to scar me for life last night.

I strut into the dressing room and the chatter amongst the girls dies down.

"Spit it out." I growl as I storm to my vanity.

"Are you going to take the job?" Queen calls out.

"Depends, if the amount of money offered offsets the fact that one of them threw a knife at me." I spit out.

"That's only happened one other time here." Tiny says as she sways to my side. "They made it worth my while, baby girl."

"They threw a knife at you, too?" I swing around in my chair.

"No," she rolls her eyes. "I had one sticking out of my tire."

"What the fuck?" I exhale and shake my head.

"They paid me more than enough to fix it." She smirks.

"Why does Raiden want to stick his knife everywhere?" I mutter and Tiny gasps.

"Raiden threw his knife at you?"

"Yes girl, I thought you got one too?" Is she stoned?

"I got one from Squall, he's the bassist and he likes 'em squishy." She taps her large breasts. "From what I know, Raiden has never chosen."

"Chosen for what?" I ask, exasperated.

"I can't talk about it." Tiny all of a sudden freezes up. "They made us sign an NDA."

"This is bullshit." I turn away from her and lift the vial from my drawer. I need to take the edge off this day.

"I told you not to do it." Sky's voice calls out.

"Fuck off." I yell at her over my shoulder.

I lean forward and sniff a line into my left nostril and lean back in my chair, letting the euphoria hit me.

"I know this is all weird to you," Sky is suddenly beside me. "There is something seriously wrong with that group. Have you heard of the Illuminati?"

"There is no such thing as the Illuminati." I roll my eyes at her.

"There is." She nods, "some celebrities join to get the success they want. Some even sell their souls."

"Look," I turn to look at her. "I agree, this shit is weird. Knife throwing or slashing tires sounds ridiculous but it kind of makes sense for these strange rock bands. But what you're saying about them being Illuminati is fucking crazy."

I lean forward again and sniff the next line into my right nostril.

"They're a metal band." Sky says on a huff.

"Same shit."

"Look them up on YouTube and see the shit they do on stage." She looks at me earnestly. "Do that before you agree to anything and look into what it means to sell your soul to the Illuminati."

"Fine." I agree so she'll just shut up and let me enjoy my high.

I give Freight my song list for the night and he watches me closely like he's expecting me to spontaneously combust. Everyone is treading carefully around me and I'd be lying if I said it wasn't making me more curious. I make a note to Google Deluge and the celebrities involved with the Illuminati when I get home.

This time on stage, I'm distracted, not hearing the beats in the music, and lost in my own thoughts of knives and men in hoodies. No amount of drugs can stop my mind's barrage of images. What is this celebration really about? Why is choosing a bunch of strippers such an ordeal? Is it really about something more nefarious?

The night pretty much continues that same way and conversations with the other girls ends up being one sided with me mostly nodding or giving one-word answers.

"Temp," Chanel snaps her fingers in my face. "We're heading out. See you tomorrow."

I wave as the girls leave the dressing room and look down at myself, I'm still fucking naked.

"Tempest." Sky calls as she pulls on her jacket. "Google them."

"Okay." I roll my eyes and begin to get dressed.

A few minutes later, I walk out the front and see Kyle cleaning around the bar, but no Freight.

"Kyle, where's Freight?"

"I think he went to hit the head. Need me to walk you out?" His arms are filled with dirty glasses and a few plates.

"Nah, I'll wait for him." I wave him off.

Freight takes a long ass time to get out of the fucking toilet, so I look out the front door and see I parked closer than I usually do. Anyways, who the fuck is still around at four in the morning? Fuck it, I decide to rush outside by myself.

I make it to my piece of shit car and roll my eyes when I realize my keys are somewhere in the bottom of my big ass purse. I open the purse, stick my hand in, and try to feel around for the irregular metal pieces. I shake my bag and crouch to the ground, opening it up wider and trying to peer inside.

"Need some help?"

I freeze at the sound of the raspy, unfamiliar voice.

"No thanks." I mutter and take a deep breath.

"You sure?"

Fear has my back breaking out into a cold sweat and my mouth drying up.

"Uh, uh." I begin to look over my shoulder but my movement is stopped by the sole of a boot.

I try to scramble forward away from the stranger but that same boot drives into my lower spine, sending me flying face first into the pavement. I roll over onto my back just as a large boot presses down onto my stomach, holding me in place. I look up to the face of an exceptionally large man whose hoodie hides his features.

"Looks like you caught something."

There are two of them, the second voice is deep, melodic, and doesn't sound like he's just smoked a whole pack of cigarettes.

"Let me up." I push at the tree trunk of a leg.

"Tempest Skeigh Verona." The second voice floats from above my head. "When I first heard it, I thought it was a unique stripper name, Tempest Skeigh. Then I find out, that is your actual name."

A hand snares into my hair, then I'm being dragged against the cement, and pulled to my feet. My head comes to the man's shoulders; I consider myself tall but he's freakishly tall. Another exceptionally large body is pressing against my back and I freeze in complete terror. I still can't make out the features of the first man but I know he's familiar. He looks a lot like one of the four men that were here last night. Deluge.

"Is this part of my choosing?" I ask quietly and the body behind me stills.

"Shouldn't have asked that." The man in front of me tsks.

A knife appears in front of my face and I open my mouth in a silent scream. I can't move, my limbs are locked, and my body is vibrating as potent terror invades all my senses.

The same all black handle and blade slowly comes at my face.

"Something inside me calls to you, Tempest." That voice washes over me and I almost moan at the captivating sound. "Your blood sings to me, tempting me to spill it, and begging me to taste it."

The edge of the blade presses against my neck and shockingly I find myself arching it to give him easier access.

"You feel that too, right? How the air around us changes, our souls pushing against our barriers, and trying to break through our skin to taste one another."

His words and that voice put me into some kind of a trance because I can feel myself languidly pushing back against him.

"Sing me a song, Tempest Skeigh Verona."

The blade cuts into the flesh of my neck, the sting instantaneous, and I can feel the slow wet trickle of blood beginning to spill down my neck. It's a surface cut, but deep enough that the blood flows unencumbered.

My head tips back on a sigh and then I feel his lips seal around the wound on my neck. I moan, the sound a little high pitched and long. Very much like a song. The soft tug on the gash sends a wash of sensation over my body and I gasp, reaching my hands up to wrap around the arm he has across my chest.

We're moving forward but I'm not paying attention until my chest and stomach hit a rough brick wall. I open my eyes and see that I've been led into the alleyway between the club and the Liquor store.

I look to the mouth of the alley and see man number one standing with his back to us, guarding us from what, I don't know. My senses begin to float back to the surface and I can feel the panic welling up inside me.

"No." I push back against the hard body behind me, "let me go."

"What's done is done, you're mine now to use as I wish." Fuck, his voice.

"What the fuck does that mean?" I question.

He pushes me back to the wall and my hands fly forward to prevent my face from meeting the unforgiving brick. I curse the decision I made today to wear a long maxi dress and a ridiculously small thong. The skirt is pulled up and over my ass, making me curse. I try to get out from between him and the coarse wall but he causes me to pause when his thumb presses into the cut on my neck. The throb from the wound and then the sound of him sucking my blood off his thumb and into his mouth, has my eyes rolling back in pleasure.

My head falls forward and rests against the brick as his hands rove over my ass.

"You're perfect," he says as his fingers pull on my thong. "You're exactly what I've been searching for."

Then that delicious mouth that acts as an outlet for that amazing voice, reseals around the laceration, his rough tongue brushing over the slice, and his fingers seeking out the wet warmth I know he'll find between my legs.

He parts my folds and my knees grow weak at his touch. His fingers slip through my arousal and circle around the hardened nub, sending arcs of lightning across my skin. I begin to moan and circle my waist, trying to create a sweet rhythm of friction for the hungry bundle of nerves he's stroking.

Then his finger pushes up into me and I groan as his knuckles scrape against my walls. I feel my pussy constrict, sucking him in further as he pushes in another, and begins to fuck me with them slowly. I'm growing louder and my pussy is sucking hungrily, the noises almost embarrassing. Almost, because right now I couldn't care less, I have never felt this way, and the orgasm that's creeping up on me is shocking.

My stomach tightens, my pussy clamps around his fingers, and my scream gets lodged in my throat as I crest the wave of my orgasm. I'm grinding into his hand when I feel a sharp pain on my right ass cheek. At first, it feels like an annoying scratching but my orgasm overpowers it and I only begin to feel the smarting sting as I come down.

He steps back, his warmth replaced with a chilling breeze, and I hear his quick intake of breath.

"Mine." He growls.

I reach my hand back, wiping along my buttock, and bringing it back to my face. I'm shocked to find it's covered in blood.

Sacrificial Lambs

TEMPEST

C.A. RENE

Chapter Five

"**W**hat the fuck?" I gasp as the bright red of my blood coats my palm.

I turn to ask this stranger what he's done when I see him already leaving the alley.

"Hey!" I drop my skirt and chase after him. "What the fuck did you do to me?"

I grab his arm and find myself quickly slammed against the brick with his hand firmly around my throat.

"Don't ever fucking touch me." He snarls, his mouth and the tip of his nose the only things visible under his hood.

"You touched me." I gasp as I try to look under the shade.

"You're mine and I can do as I wish with you. Your body is mine, your breath is mine, and your dark, cold soul is mine." I close my eyes at the sound of his voice, feeling myself become calmer than any drug has given me.

"Raiden." I whisper his name, it must be him.

He has a goatee that curves around his full round lips, the color black with a sprinkling of gray throughout and his nose is slightly wide, one nostril sporting two rings while the other has a single stud. His tongue comes out to wet his bottom lip and I see a small bar through the tip. I want to know how it would feel to have that bar gliding against my pussy and sinking deep inside.

Fuck.

I try to shake off the stupor I keep finding myself in and sort out my thoughts.

"Why did you cut me?"

His hand squeezes tighter around my throat and his plump lips pull back and tighten against his bright white teeth, "You. Are. Mine."

His body crowds in against mine and the coarse brick begins to dig into my back, his mouth so close to mine. I want his kiss and the feel of his breath washing over my face has me wishing we could get closer still.

Then, he breaks away and I whimper at the absence of his touch. He turns his back and walks away from me like he didn't just violate me in the best way. I continue to lean against the wall, catching my breath, and feeling the sting on my ass and neck. I need about four Valium and twelve hours of sleep.

I push off the wall and swiftly walk back to my car, my ass smarting and the blood running down my leg. I'm starting to see why Sky was so fucking scared of these men. As much as I want to sleep, I need to get home and Google Deluge.

Once home, my slow as fuck laptop hums loudly like it's ready to take off and I pour myself a large glass of wine. The pain in my ass has eased but the skin is an ugly red color and inflamed around a long, jagged cut. I cleaned the wound and covered it with a bandage because the sight of my broken skin makes me want to fucking lose it.

I pull up Google and type in Deluge. A bunch of articles pop up but it's the first picture that has my full attention. All of them in what looks to be long black robes, the hoods wide and low over their heads, and their mouths on full display. I intuitively know which one is Raiden, the shape of those lips will forever be ingrained in my mind, and I touch my neck on the cut he licked clean.

The others are pretty much normal save for the long, pointed beards and is that a forked tongue?! One of them has a forked tongue! I scroll over the articles and there are a few that stand out from the late nineties.

"Deluge causes a riot in the streets of Chicago."

"They're at it again! Deluge Kills a dove on stage."

"Blood thrown onto the crowd! Deluge being fined."

"Is Deluge really a part of the Illuminati?"

That last one gives me pause and I quickly open the link. There's a picture of the four of them looking much younger and a lot more out of control, the picture is grainy with how old it is so I can't really pick out their features. But they're all topless and muscular like running backs. Two of them have their hands thrown up and their fingers shaped into a triangle.

"Deluge greeted fans backstage tonight after their final concert for the tour. When a fan asked them what the secret to their success was, lead singer Raiden James said, quote, 'hard work and a lot of blood.' To which his bandmate Torrent added 'sweat and tears, too.' Strange right? Especially when they draw Illuminati symbols from dove's blood onto the stage during their shows. Then let's not forget their very own manager Kenny Tonga has been known to associate with many suspected Illuminati members."

Okay, so these guys sound a bit fucked up, like a lot a bit and my stinging ass can attest to that. My satisfied pussy on the other hand, wants more of the fucking madness. I can't help but be somewhat drawn to the man that tasted my blood and finger fucked me simultaneously.

Next, I Google the Illuminati and skim through a few sites but not really learning much. There's nothing about selling souls to the devil but there is an in-depth explanation about secret societies and that we may never know exactly what the Illuminati are or what they stand for.

I hit a link to a YouTube video and one of their songs begins to play. It's heavy metal with the angry sounding electric guitar and the hard crashing of drums, but Raiden's voice is singing like it's Sunday choir. He sounds beautiful against the aggressive background noise and his voice is melodic.

I close the laptop and sit back on the couch. I'm intrigued and if I'm being honest with myself, I have always been slightly attracted to the more fucked up things in life. That includes the men I choose, too. Hence why I'm sitting here in this one room apartment and pulling my clothes off every night for a buck. I'm not your average twenty-one-year-old.

For as long as I can remember, everything that surrounded me was different shades of dark and I grew up thinking that was normal. People weren't nice, life was hard, and survival meant you made it another day.

Anything more than that was a privilege, which I rarely had.

Maybe if I had a mother that stuck around to raise me, things would've been different, I was about six when she left, but I can't seem to summon her face or hear her voice, and she's long been forgotten. I have been told many different versions of the same story and they all add up to the same conclusion, she was a cunt who left her young daughter in the hands of an alcoholic father.

I know nothing of her family, where she came from, and where she went. My father was rarely sober and asking about her always resulted in more questions than answers. He resented her for leaving and even more for sticking him with me. Not that he raised me, I was left to the streets most days, and that meant I was stealing food and robbing people's pockets.

That's why I'm sitting here, sucking back a bottle of wine, and wincing whenever I shift on my ass, instead of crying at a police station. I don't trust pigs and I know in most cases they cause a bigger problem instead of solving it.

I know I can handle the likes of Deluge because this shit isn't new to me and men like Raiden are more familiar than not. Like he said, my soul is cold and dark, and I know there's no light at the end of the tunnel around here.

I chug down the rest of the bottle and let the glass hit the carpet, watching as it rolls towards a few others. Raiden may think he owns me but he has no idea what owning me entails.

I am looking forward to watching him find out.

Sacrificial Lambs

TEMPEST

C.A. RENE

Chapter Six

"arl," I slam my fists against my hips. "Him and his goon jumped me as I was heading to my car."

"Why were you alone?" His brows crash together in confusion.

"Who the fuck cares?" I throw my hands up. "They fucking jumped me and that crazy motherfucker carved into my skin."

I tip my head to show him my neck and then turn to lift the skirt I'm wearing, giving him a good view of the long, jagged cut in my ass cheek.

"I wanted you to stay home." He drops his head into his hands. "Then maybe this could have been avoided."

"I can't stay home!" I yell. "I need to work."

"Now, you're in his sights, there's nothing I can do." He leans back in his chair. "You can leave this place."

"Leave?" I widen my eyes.

"Yeah, I don't know that he wouldn't hunt you down though, I think he'd enjoy that."

"I'm not leaving because some old asshole Illuminati bitch is trying to scare me." I turn on my heel and stomp towards his office door.

"Tempest, I wouldn't say that shit to anyone else if I were you," he calls to my back. "They are coming tonight for the choosing. Be ready."

"Fuck them," I flip him the bird over my shoulder. "And fuck their fucking choosing."

Tonight's line up consists of me, Queen, Diamond, and Tiny. I think Tiny requested this night hoping Squall would choose her again. She said it was an amazing experience and a lot of money was transferred into her account afterward.

I won't be hitting the stage tonight, the cut on my ass is ugly and I can only imagine what the girls would be saying about it. Instead, I sit at the bar with Kyle and guzzle back all the free drinks he rolls to me. I can see the interest in his eyes but I can say with one-hundred percent certainty that he stirs absolutely nothing in me.

"Not going on tonight?" He asks me.

"Nope." I shake my head and down the tequila shot, flicking the lime slice back at him.

"Shame, I like watching you the most." He grins what he must think is his panty dropping grin.

"I bet." I wink and suddenly my back is hot as a body steps up to it.

I know who it is, it's the same energy as last night, and I watch as Kyle scurries off down the bar like the pussy he is.

"You carved into my ass like a fucking thanksgiving turkey, you asshole." I snarl my back still to him.

"Is that why you're not dancing?"

Fuck me, that voice.

"I'm damaged enough on the inside, I'm not feeling like displaying the now damaged outside." I cross my arms over my chest.

"Do you want to never dance here again?" His breath hits my neck and I shiver from its warmth.

"Are you going to whisk me away and give me a

better life?" I snort.

"No," he chuckles and the sound goes straight to my clit.

I turn to confront him but once again see his back as he walks towards a table filled with the other band members and their manager. All of them wear hoods, save for the cunt in a suit, and all of them are looking my way. Raiden sits in the booth and leans back, his legs opening wide. His fingers begin to curl the hairs on his chin and my mouth waters when I remember where they were early this morning.

My reaction to him is nothing short of visceral and from the smirks of his bandmates, they notice it too. The only one not smirking is their manager, he's looking at me like I'm unworthy, and his brow lifts as if to ask why am I still looking? I flip him the bird and turn back around on my stool. He doesn't intimidate me but he is dredging up these feelings of not being good enough.

I hop down from my stool and make my way back to the dressing room. I'm inebriated from alcohol but alcohol stopped being enough a long time ago. Now I need something stronger, something more chemical to stop myself from succumbing to everything I've failed to deal with.

"I have to do three dances tonight." Diamond moans from the vanity beside me.

"Sorry girl," I shrug as I cut my lines into the glass top. "I had an accident and I don't think men want to see a bloody bandage on stage."

She looks at me skeptically but I don't give a fuck. Diamond is a girl who grew up with a lot of money and this is her big rebellion to her pretentious family. She's pretty enough, but her face always holds that haughty sneer rich people inherit. Her hair is a dirty blonde and her eyes a bright green. She's average height and her body is still all soft curves, showcasing her lack of work and young age.

"I was asked to come tonight." She lights a cigarette and I scrunch my face at the smell. I hate cigarettes. "Looks like I might be working at some private party."

"Were you given a knife?" I ask her.

"What?" She looks from me to the coke on my table.

"Nevermind."

"Carl asked me to come." She flips back her hair with a grin on her face.

She's had a thing for Carl for a while now and I find it amusing when he barely acknowledges her. He's easily fifteen years older than her but whatever, all girls find themselves crushing on an older man at some point in their lives. I've had a few myself.

"Diamond." Freight calls "You're up."

I turn to look at Freight and his jaw is clenched as he purposely ignores me.

"I'm sorry about not waiting for you to walk me last night." I tell him, I'm not sure how much Carl has told him.

"That could've been dangerous, Tempest." His deep voice growls. "You could've been grabbed. Do you know the type of men that watch you?"

Okay, so he knows nothing about what happened.

"I know, I won't do it again." I tell him as he gives me a short nod and walks Diamond to the stage.

I'm finally alone in the dressing room. Diamond is about to do her set, Queen is walking the tables, and

Tiny is doing a private dance down the hall. I lean back in my chair and breathe in deep, I can feel something is coming, something different, and something life altering. It's there just floating beyond my reach and I'm ready to leap forward.

"You should wear your leather number, the dominatrix one." Carl says.

"Okay." I shrug, "I can't dance tonight, did you want me at the tables?"

"Nah, Queen got it. Just get ready." He raps his knuckles on the door and then walks back towards his office.

I begin to pull my hair back into a high pony and decide on dark smokey makeup, might as well look as dark as I feel.

The lights are dimmed, the doors are locked, and these five men line the edge of the stage. They want to see us dance, watch us entertain, and see if we are good enough for the likes of Deluge.

"Tiny is up next and she'll be dancing to Pony by Ginuwine." Mouth announces and I try hard not to roll my eyes at the most obvious song.

Tiny blows us all a kiss and struts to the front and grabs the pole. Tiny is all curves but she works them perfectly to the beat. She does her number and even I'm a little hot and bothered when she comes strolling back to us in nothing but a string up her ass.

"Diamond will be dancing to Candy Shop by 50 Cent." Mouth calls out and I can't stop the groan that escapes my mouth.

Diamond shoots me a look before she heads out to the front of the stage. She begins her dance and I watch as Raiden leans forward, resting his arms on the glossy wooden surface. He's not looking at her, I can tell his eyes are trained on me, and that hood does nothing to hide it.

"Queen is up and she will be dancing to London Bridge by Fergie."

Queen claps her hands and skips out to the pole. London Bridge? Really? She's been stripping this long and she picks London Bridge? I close my eyes and still feel the heat of his glare.

"Tempest Skeigh is up and she's dancing to Swim by Chase Atlantic."

My body goes on autopilot as I slowly walk to the pole. My hips sway in time with the music as I slowly start to pull the zipper down my chest, I grab for the pole and hoist myself up, spinning around it seductively.

Raiden slowly straightens from the stage and I can see his jawline under the hood tighten. I don't have any skin showing in this leather ensemble since it's a full catsuit and that suits me because of the still inflamed cut on my ass.

My feet touch the stage again and I pivot to face the five men in front of me. I have nothing underneath and the sweat collecting between my breasts begins to roll down my stomach. I lick my lips, close my eyes, and rotate my hips as I work the zipper down to my belly button. My breasts strain against the leather and I begin to pull it open.

"Enough." His voice cuts through all music and straight through my chest, making my heart sputter. "You were already chosen. There's no need for you to dance."

I look down at him and quirk my brow, why is he really interrupting my dance?

"I think we already got an idea of how you move last night." The guy to Raiden's right chuckles.

"Oh yeah?" I say to him as I lower myself to a squat, meeting him hood to eye. "When do you start cutting everyone else open and tasting their blood? Is it that particular move you're talking about?"

He doesn't answer me and I smirk as I rise back to standing. I won't be afraid of a bunch of old guys still trapped in their golden era. They can hop from club to club looking for strippers all they want, they're still just a bunch of has-beens.

I walk back to the lineup and stand there with my chest still exposed. I cross my arms and look to Carl with my brow raised. What now?

"We're missing someone." The suit calls out. "Someone else was chosen."

"Sorry Kenny, who else?" Carl strides forward. That's the suit's name and the band's manager, Kenny Tonga.

"Hail chose Sky." Kenny says.

"Sky hasn't been in for the last few days." Carl stutters a bit. "I'll call her."

"See that you do."

Then we all stand there and watch as Kenny turns and starts for the exit with his band following single file, all but Raiden. He points his finger at me and then curls it towards him, beckoning me to him. It's like a string is connected from that finger to my soul because I walk to him without thought.

He drops his hood and I suck in a breath when

I see his face. He's breathtaking and I don't mean that in the pretty sense. No, Raiden is dark and devastatingly breathtaking. His skin is the shade of sepia, silky, and decadent looking. His eyes are a unique blend of light green and gold, shining bright against his skin tone. Dark, thick lashes extend from his eyelids and nearly touch his eyebrows. His nose has the piercings on display and those lips, so sinful as he smirks.

I squat down so we are face to face and those eyes lock mine into place. I open my mouth to say something when his hand fastens around my throat, pulling me in.

"Did you misunderstand me when I said you were mine?" I want to moan at the sound of his voice but I swallow it down.

I shake my head, still staring into those eyes, and unable to look away.

"That includes your body, the skin wrapped around it, and the blood pumping through it. All. Fucking. Mine." His fingers tighten and my eyes widen when I can no longer suck in air. "Do I need to carve into this face to make my point?"

I shake my head again and he removes his hand. I clutch at my throat while gasping for air and he chuckles.

"I'll see you soon." He says as he pulls his hood back up and follows the rest of his group through the exit doors.

My insides quake with uncertainty but my pussy is soaking with anticipation.

SING ME a Song

Sacrificial Lambs

TEMPEST

C.A. RENE

Chapter Seven

The ceiling is spinning as I squint my eyes and try to focus on one spot. As soon as I came home, I grabbed the bottle of vodka and guzzled almost half in one shot. I'll see you soon. As ominous as it sounds, I can't help but wonder how long is soon, and will it involve more of what happened in that alley-minus the skin carving.

Speaking of, after my shower I stood there and stared at the laceration. It looks like a lightning bolt or three sevens from top to bottom. I'll be lucky if it doesn't scar because the cuts are deep. I roll over and groan when the room rolls with me, maybe a glass of water is needed.

I get up and stumble my way into the kitchen area, hitting a few objects on the way. I pull open the small fridge, grab a bottle of water, and something catches my eye by the one and only window in this shithole. It's raining heavily but I swear I can make out a figure standing about a yard away by the tree.

I rush to the window in my drunken stupor, almost hitting the glass, and pull the curtains closed. Did I actually see someone or was I imagining it? After the past few days dealing with Deluge and all the secrecy bullshit behind them, I can see why I would be imagining shit. That and vodka make for a terrible combo.

I stagger back to my bed and fall face first into the pillows.

My mouth feels like I ate a pot of dirt and dipped it in a pile of shit. My head is pounding and my bladder is protesting. Fuck me and my impulsive decisions to drown in bottles of whatever I can find.

I roll out of bed and head to the bathroom, I need to wash the stench of alcohol off me. I need to speak to Sky today and ask her why the fuck she didn't tell me she was chosen, too. She is obviously trying to avoid these guys but it doesn't look like they're going to let her and I can only imagine how fucking scared she is.

I get myself ready for work and step out of my apartment, lock the door, and jog down the narrow stairs that lead to the parking lot. The sun has long ago set and the lights for the lot are mostly out, so I don't see the black limo until it's too late.

"Miss Verona. I will be taking you to your destination." A tall man in a chauffeur's suit says as he opens the door.

"Like fuck you will, old man-"

"Temp, get in here." Sky's voice cuts me off and I bend to look inside the limo.

She's sitting in the far corner with a pair of shades on her face and an oversized hoodie on her slight frame. I do as she says and slide in beside her.

"What the fuck is this?" I watch as she opens the mini fridge and pulls out a champagne bottle. I gag a little because of my hangover but my hand still reaches for the bottle.

"We're being taken to them." She mutters.

"Excuse you?" I ask as I tip back the bottle.

"Deluge, this is their limo." She rests her head against the seat.

"How the fuck you not gonna tell me you were chosen?" I snarl at her.

"I was chosen last year, too." She moans and turns her head to the window. "I worked at a different club, they came by, and I ended up with a knife stuck into my vanity."

I continue to gulp back the champagne, waiting for her to continue.

"I ran out. I heard things, Temp. I read things and fuck, I watched videos. They do crazy shit on stage and they are known Illuminati members, it really fucking freaks me out. What's up with all this choosing shit? Ya know?"

"True." I nod. It is all fucking strange.

"I laid low for a bit then found this job here at The Temple." She huffs. "But now they're here."

"Did Hail choose you last time, too?" I ask her.

"Yeah." She mutters and grabs the bottle back. "This time his knife was stuck into my mother's front door."

Fuck. That's a serious veiled threat and I can see why she's scared.

I look out the window and see that we are going in the opposite direction as the club. We head straight for Manhattan and my heart once again picks up speed.

"We're going to their office, I would assume." Sky says as she watches me begin to freak out. "According to Tiny, they bring everyone here first to sign NDAs and to agree to the terms."

"You have a choice Sky, you can decline the

offer."

"Do I?" Her big brown eyes focus on me. "He stuck a knife in my mother's door. Did you Google them like I told you? Did you not see how fucked up they are?"

Do we have a choice? I want to say yes, of course we have a choice because that's the way life should be, but I think back to that alley and to last night. No, we don't have a fucking choice. Tiny went to one of these things and she said she liked it, fuck she's trying to get there again this year. Can it really be that bad dancing for a bunch of old guys?

The drive is about thirty minutes and we pull up to a glass building, the moon and stars reflecting off its surface.

"This building belongs to Deluge?"

"No, this is their management company's building." Sky answers as the driver gets out and opens the door.

We both get out and look up the length of the skyscraper. The towering frame is intimidating, just like its occupants, and I pull my jacket tighter around me.

"Let's get this the fuck over with." She growls as she storms towards a set of double doors. There's no name on this building, nothing to indicate ownership whatsoever.

The door opens before she reaches it and another guy waves her inside, he looks over to me with a raised brow.

"How the fuck do I get myself into these situations?" I mutter and follow Sky.

I walk through the door and find Sky sitting on a couch with a few other girls. There's about ten of us in here and one I recognize besides me and Sky. Diamond.

"Hey girls." She smirks.

"Shut the fuck up." Sky snaps at her and I cough to hide my laugh.

"I'm so excited to be here." Diamond gushes to the girl beside her. "I love Deluge's music. I grew up with their music playing in my household."

"If you will follow me ladies." A woman stands from the front desk.

All the girls follow her and I end up being the last one, dragging my feet. She leads us down one corridor and then we turn into another. I see the different record plaques on the wall, platinum, diamonds, golds…

A hand appears from a darkened office and I'm yanked inside. Before I can scream, a hand covers my mouth, and I'm shoved against the wall.

This feels all too familiar.

TEMPEST

C.A. RENE

Chapter Eight

Raiden.

I know it's him without seeing him because my brain has marked his scent as unique and familiar. He's pressed against my back, pushing me into the wall, and his nose hits my neck.

"I was hoping you wouldn't show." His voice is low and melodic. "I wanted to hunt you down, drag you here, and then punish you."

His other hand grabs onto my ass-right over the cut-and squeezes. I whimper as pain skates up my back and down my leg. He rips down my leggings and slaps his hand to the cut, then chuckles when I yell into his hand.

"That's going to be a gorgeous scar."

I struggle until he lets me go and I shove him off me, pulling my pants back up. I turn to face him and step in closer to his body.

He doesn't have his hood up today and even though it's dark in here, I can still see his features. His hair is cropped short but I can see the gray at his temples, his eyes sparkle with a sinister look, and his luscious mouth is curved into a wicked smirk.

"Punish me how?" What?

His brows raise with surprise and he barks out a dark sounding laugh.

"Something that would involve your blood running over your skin and into my mouth."

Well.

"You think you're a vampire or something?" I cross my arms. "Too much acid during your heyday?"

"Blood is a person's life force." Fuck, his voice. "You can learn a lot about them when you drink their vitality."

"That's fucked up." I shake my head.

He licks his lips and bites down on the bottom one, making my thighs clench. Then he steps into me and I drop my arms from my chest just to feel him.

"Do you want to know what I learned about you, Tempest?" I want to moan when he says my name.

"Yes." I answer on a whisper as his mouth lowers closer to mine.

"You're sad, you have a bottomless depth to your pain, and you're weak." His breath fans my face and even though his words are harsh, he's right.

"Fuck you." It comes out sounding weak. "Was it you outside my apartment last night?"

His face turns dark and he completely ignores my question. "Go back into the hall and enter the last door on the right. Sign the paperwork, Tempest, and I will help you soar past all of that."

I want him to kiss me. He's standing so close and his mouth is right there...

He pulls back and turns me around, "go."

I open the door, step out, and slam it shut behind me. I hear his chuckle inside and roll my eyes, I'm in so much fucking trouble. I can feel all things nefarious when I'm near him and yet my body wants his.

I get to the door he stated and see the girls standing in a line leading to a desk. Sitting at the desk is Kenny himself and he's handing out envelopes to each of them.

Looks thick and again I try to shake some sense into my head. Why would a birthday party need all this? These guys aren't popular anymore, TMZ wouldn't care about them, and it doesn't look like girls are trying to chase them down.

"Where the fuck were you?" Sky clamps her fingers into my forearm and hauls me to her side.

I shrug and look straight ahead.

"Be careful." She hisses and snatches the envelope out of Kenny's hand.

The look on his face is comical, he's looking at her like she's grown an extra head, and I can't control the giggle that escapes.

"Ah, Tempest Skeigh Verona." He gives me a disgusted once over. "That is an interesting name. It means storm."

"I know that." I huff as I grab onto the envelope. His grip stays firm and he looks into my eyes. "Don't get too attached."

I pull on the envelope and he lets it go with a smirk. I sit down beside Sky on the couch and pull out the contents of the envelope. There is indeed an NDA inside that clearly states anything that happens during this weeklong excursion is never repeated again. A week?! The next page is an agreement to fly on a chartered jet to an undisclosed destination of the band's choice. What the fuck? I won't even know where I'm going until I get there.

The energy in the room changes, like something cold but electrifying has entered, and my hair on the back of my neck stands. Raiden is here. I don't bother to look up and instead read the next page that says I will be paid a cool thirty G's for this gig.

I choke on my saliva and drop the papers to the floor. Sky barely lifts her head to look at me and shakes it subtly. Is this shit for real? They are paying ten girls thirty thousand to shake their asses for a week? Fucking sign me up!

I pick up the papers and stride over to the desk where Kenny and Raiden have their heads close together and speaking low.

"I need a pen." I say to Kenny, not once looking at Raiden.

"Don't you think you should read all the fine print?" Kenny has that grimy smirk on his face.

"My life has never been based on the fine print and I'm not going to start now."

Raiden chuckles and hands me a pen. Our fingers touch as I grab it and I gasp at the electric current that courses up my arm. His smile drops and his eyebrows crash together in a look of frustration.

"I should ask for your signature in blood." He mutters as he turns and storms out of the office.

"Still sure you don't want to read the fine print?" Kenny sneers.

His face pisses me off, so I throw the papers down on his desk, and bend over to sign each one.

"Are you sure you picked the right girl?" I sneer back at him and stuff the papers back in the envelope.

"Oh, I'm sure, Tempest Skeigh Verona."

SING ME a Song

Sacrificial Lambs

RAIDEN

C.A. RENE

Chapter Nine

There's something that simmers just under the surface of her skin that sings to my fucking soul. I want to cut her open and watch it all seep out of her.

The feeling is so strong and I have to focus all my attention on not stabbing her jugular just so I can breathe again.

That first night I watched her dance on the stage in nothing but that fur abomination, I knew she was something special, and since then it's been hard to stay away. I hate that she's being dragged into this because I can see the strength hidden there under her pain.

The night Torrent and I watched her leave that piece of shit club and run to her car wasn't planned. I didn't want to approach her, I didn't want to touch her but I lost all common sense and my instincts took over. She looked weak, she looked scared, and she looked tantalizing.

I can still see those stormy grey eyes narrowing in anger as I dismissed her, those eyes portray everything, and the pain that shines through them is fucking delectable. I can see why they wanted her there and why I had to be the one to choose her.

I storm down the corridor and into my office, slamming the door shut behind me. When her skin brushed against mine, I had the overwhelming need to kill something just to stave off the craving for more of her touch. I will not get attached to her, there can be no sentiment associated with the dark-haired demon.

It's a fucking shame because I have never been this drawn to anybody before and now her life is in my very hands.

"What's up your ass?"

I turn at the sound of Torrent's voice and throw myself into my chair. Torrent is my blood brother, our parents were drug addicts, and both died of overdoses when we were younger. We both ended up in an orphanage and when I turned sixteen to his fourteen, we ran off. A few years later, we started Deluge and we haven't looked back.

"Nothing." I crack my neck.

"You saw her, didn't you?"

I give him a brief nod and lean back. "I don't know how I'm going to last the week with her."

"Good thing you won't have to see her after that." He chuckles and snorts the line he's cut up on my desk.

"I think someone's watching her." I mumble.

"Probably Kenny," he shrugs.

"I can only hope that after this year, we'll be done with this shit and moving on to the next group." I scrub my hand down my face.

"I can't wait to see the look on Kenny's face when it all goes down." Torrent laughs.

"He brought us into this mess, it's only right he sees us out of it."

"Revenge will taste so fucking sweet." Torrent laughs.

"Yeah." I mumble and turn to look out the window. "Did yours show up?"

"Of course, that bitch was eager." He chuckles

and stands. "Hail and I are heading out to get everything we need for mass. Do you need anything?"

I shake my head and a few seconds later the door opens and shuts.

The thought of my birthday is exhausting and the age I'm turning probably has a lot to do with it.

Forty-five.

Age means nothing to me, it's how I feel on the inside and my insides are brimming with youth. It's my mind that's exhausted. I carry this group, I lead us with an iron fist, and sometimes their faces feel just how iron it is. My birthday used to be a cause for excitement and anticipation, but now I just want to get it over with.

I'm getting restless as I pour over details, making sure everything is exactly right, and keeping our manager in the dark. This is by far the largest group of them yet and the original four who coerced us to sign our names in blood, taking advantage of our young age and jaded pasts.

There is one thing I'm looking forward to and it's the one thing I have been cursing myself for. I pull out the switchblade in my pocket and open it up. There are still a few brown spots of her dried blood on the blade and I run my tongue along its sharpened edge, risking the slice to taste her again.

I wasn't lying when I told her she tasted of pain and weakness, but there was something I left out. Her blood was flavored like sin and that is the part that calls to me. I have never had something so weak and yet so sinful.

My cock swells in my pants and I grab it as my tongue envelopes the tip of the blade. Soon enough, I will have her at my mercy, her body to do with as I please, and those eyes to stare into as long as I want. When I've had my fill, I'll be more than ready to let her go.

SING ME a Song

Sacrificial Lambs

TEMPEST

C.A. RENE

Chapter Ten

The club is packed tonight, and I am still shook over the fact that in a few hours I will be boarding a jet to an unknown destination to earn thirty grand. It's an answer to so many of my problems. Does it clear all my debt? No, but it will certainly chop it down to normal standards.

I've just finished my set and I'm waiting for Sky to finish up hers, then we're going to leave here and head to the address that was sent to us via text this morning. I may be excited to earn all this money in what I hope will be an exotic locale but I also feel trepidation towards all the secrets and seeing Raiden again.

My mind has been held hostage the last few days since I saw him and my body replays every spot he's touched me.

"You girls are so lucky." Tiny moans from her vanity.

"I know." Diamond says, her voice dripping with disdain.

"I'm sorry you didn't get chosen this year." I say to her and she gives me a small smile.

I saw the girl that Squall had chosen this time and she's also a gorgeous plus size dancer from another club.

"Verona." Carl calls from the doorway. "My office."

I feel like telling him to fuck off but quite frankly,

thirty grand still ain't enough to walk out on my job. Besides, Carl hasn't done anything to me but be kind and give me a job.

He's sitting at his desk when I get there and I close the door behind me.

"What's up?" I ask and he looks up at me.

"I need you to sign this form before you leave today." He shoves a piece of paper across the desk.

I read it and laugh out loud. It's basically something that states I chose of my own free will to participate at this event and in no way did The Temple have anything to do with it.

"This is all starting to sound like if I die, then none of y'all can be sued." I look into his wide eyes. "Do I need to know something?"

"It's because you are leaving the country with a group of men to do a private party. You met those men in my club and if anything happens to you overseas, I do not need the police breathing down my neck."

"Gotcha." I sign my name on the dotted line.

I turn to leave his office and hear him clear his throat.

"Take care, Temp."

"Thanks Carl." I grin over my shoulder and exit the office.

When I get back to the dressing room, Chanel is there looking through a few of my outfits.

"Can I help you?" I ask and she spins around.

"I figure you're gonna be gone all week, might as well put a few of these to good use." She stumbles over her words.

"Don't touch my shit." I snarl at her as she scurries by me.

"Let's get out of here." Sky struts in with her tits bouncing and her braids swinging. "I need this week to go by as fast as most men fuck."

I snort and grab up my two duffle bags as she throws on a sweatsuit. I don't mind this weeklong excursion and no matter how hard I try to deny it, I don't mind seeing Raiden again either.

We're dropped off at a small airport and led to a landing strip that has a large jet, its stairs descended to the asphalt. I see a few of the other girls giggling as they jog up them and a few others loitering to the side smoking cigarettes.

There seems to be about twelve of us and I can't help the excitement that courses through me. I want to go somewhere exotic because I never thought I would be able to, growing up dirt poor in a trailer will do that to you. I want to experience this even if it is at the hands of a man whose very pores sing with evil.

I'm following closely behind Sky who's muttering curses and shaking her head around. I know she doesn't want to do this and I get that her being here is completely due to her protecting her mother. We start up the stairs and I gasp as I get the first glimpse of the inside of the jet.

The seats look like the softest butter and the floor is a rich crimson red. There are red curtains over each of the small windows and the lights glow all different colors along the aisle floor. This is a luxury I have never witnessed in my life. Laying across one of the butter soft couches is Diamond.

She has a champagne flute in one hand and a bowl of grapes resting on her lap. She gives us a sly look and a smarmy grin.

"Hey girls. Come aboard." She pops a grape into

her mouth.

Her voice and face drips with arrogance and it's grating on my last fucking nerve.

"I'm only going to tell you this one more time." Sky bends down into her face. "Shut the fuck up."

I snort as I follow Sky to another two-seater and watch as Diamond's face screws up into a sneer. She may be one to cause us issues, and I know I will have to keep an eye on Sky around her. Especially if Sky decides to drink, then she's even mouthier, and I can only foresee problems between them.

I look around the jet, seemingly taking in its opulence, but I'm looking for him. The man that's old enough to be my father but will not leave my mind. There's something that seems so youthful about him regardless of how old he looks.

I breathe out my disappointment when I notice that neither him nor his bandmates are on this jet and I still don't have a clue where we're going.

"If everyone will board the plane and take your seats. We can get going." The stewardess calls out.

"Where are we even going?" Diamond's pretentious voice calls out.

"To Hell, bitch." Sky mutters and I laugh into my hand.

"We will be going to the Caribbean island of Dominica." The stewardess smiles wide.

Huh? I have never heard of Dominica.

"Of course." Sky leans her head back and closes her eyes.

"What's in Dominica?" I ask her.

"Myths and volcanoes."

RAIDEN

C.A. RENE

Chapter Eleven

"Embrace the chaos inside of you, for this makes you wise, and perfection can only be found through the most chaotic. Elevate above the mortal plane and its simplistic form of thought. Do whatever you need to accomplish all your desires."

"Yes, Magus." The four of us mutter in synchrony.

"Go and spread your seed for it is great, spill blood for it is revered, and worship only yourself for you are your own god."

"Yes, Magus." We repeat.

"Go and be in his darkness."

We all rise from our crossed legged positions on four points of the pentagram and Kenny drops his hood from where he's standing at the fifth point. His cloak is pitch black with a royal purple lining and the symbol of Baphomet on the front. Only the best for a priest of the dark one.

"How many this year?" Kenny asks as he removes his cloak.

"The magisters requested four." I answer him.

"Including Tempest." His knowing smirk pisses me off.

"As you wanted." I nod once.

"Four this year will bring you back into favor with the magisters, then maybe we can work on that new album." Kenny says.

That's what happens when you're young and salivating for fame and fortune, you agree to absurd terms for it and choose to ignore the darker requirements. Our commitment now belongs to a secret group that believes all great things move in the dark. Too bad we have become the most dangerous things moving in that dark now and we have our own fucking plans.

"Everything is planned, Magus." Torrent interjects. "We should get going because the girls have already taken off."

Squall and Hail nod as Kenny looks between all of us. He touches each of our heads and then nods his dismissal.

"I will see you all soon."

I follow the guys out of Kenny's house and breathe in the calming air. I need to get to Dominica and I need to get my hands on the girl whose face hasn't left my mind in days. It's a first for me and I can't decipher if it's because I'm craving her defiance or I want my dick inside of her.

This will be a weeklong affair of challenging my demon and fucking every orifice on her body.

"Let's get on this fucking plane." Torrent growls as he dips his pinky nail into a baggie of coke, then hands it to me.

I do the same, taking a few bumps into each nostril. I am going to need to take the edge off this anticipation I feel. I have been disciplined and I won't let that be destroyed by a girl with hair like a raven and eyes like the storm her name represents.

"This abstinence rule before our leader's birthday is fucking cruel." Squall moans as he grabs his cock through his jeans.

"It's for one fucking week." Hail shoves at him and we all chuckle.

Squall is an addict of a different sort. Sure, he likes drugs and partakes in alcohol but he needs sex. His dick being in anyone erases the jumble of thoughts in his mind and helps him forget his past. It's not healthy but none of us are remotely healthy.

We work hard to make our lives a success, to live in luxury, and to achieve all our desires. It doesn't fucking matter how we get there, as long as we do in the end. And we always fucking get there.

Our success came from sacrifices, our own, and plenty from the other members. Sacrifice is the key to all answers and we sacrifice everything for our own gain. When we joined this organization, this one rule was beaten into us and it's one that will stay with us until we die. It's the reason none of us are married or have families and we never will. We are our own most important entity and no one else can come before ourselves. No one, not even the very people that brought us into the fold.

Our boundaries are each other and as the band's leader, I make sure we stay on the right path. Therefore, every year we use my birthday as our thanks to the ones that set us free, that led us from the over searing light and into the safety of the dark. It's our time to indulge in all the power we possess and to show we are grateful. I can't fucking wait to show the magisters and our very own Magus just how grateful we are.

"The orphanage burnt down last week." Hail states quietly and we all stop to look at him. "They said it was faulty wiring."

"Sounds like someone went back and did what

we were all wanting to do eventually." Torrent snarls, his pupils the size of pinpricks.

We are all from the same orphanage and the place was run by Catholic nuns that liked to forget their vows of celibacy when we were alone. Even the Catholic priests that came for Sunday services liked to make sure we boys swallowed every drop of the lord's grace.

No wonder we were so quick to jump on the bus leading us to the other side of religion, and quick to drop the ones preaching about the light but committing the darkest crimes. We no longer wanted to praise a lord that took that praise in the form of raping young kids.

"The kids?" I ask.

"Twenty-three dead including four nuns. Sister Jane was among them." Hail says quietly.

Ah, sister Jane. She liked to whip us when we misbehaved then fuck us with the whip's handle after, just to drive home our sins. She was the evilest, some would say that she was the fucking devil.

"Then let's be thankful for their sacrifice in ridding the Earth of Sister Jane." I nod and the others do the same.

Like I said, sacrifice is the key to all answers.

Sacrificial Lambs

TEMPEST

C.A. RENE

Chapter Twelve

Dominica.

It's breathtaking here, the trees are a lush green, and the ocean is a sparkling clear turquoise. I have never seen anything like it. We are staying in a large mansion that easily has twenty rooms and as Sky and I were wandering around, we found a ballroom of sorts along with a large dining room.

There's a staff that comes at regular intervals with drinks and food, and a cook came to announce our dinner this evening, duck, and vegetables. I've never had duck, growing up, I was lucky if I had chicken to go with my ramen noodles.

"Did you read the itinerary in your room?" Sky asks as she downs her third glass of wine.

"I did." We have tonight off to settle in but starting tomorrow evening from five pm onward, we are to be present for all festivities.

"Let's take advantage of this free time and get drunk."

She's acting like this is a hard gig and it's starting to grate on my nerves. This is easy work and the pay is well and above premium. I decide to get up and start mingling with the other girls. Why not make friends with some girls that are as excited to be here as me?

I see a group of three girls, all blonde, tall, and willowy standing around the bar. I head to them and they smile when I approach.

"Hey." I give a short awkward wave and they all chuckle. "I'm Tempest."

"Nice stage name." One girl says and the others nod.

"It's my stage name and actual name." I grin and roll my eyes.

"Sweet. I'm Nova and this is Lavender and Silk." Nova points to the other girls. "We're a little nervous and about to take some shots, you in?"

"Yes!" I grin and watch as Nova pulls out a bottle of Patron.

My eyes open to complete darkness and I try to decipher why my heart is beating wildly. What woke me up out of a dead, alcohol induced slumber?

"You look like an angel when you sleep," I gasp at his voice. "Such a vast difference from the demon you resemble during the day."

"Raiden?" I sit up in bed and the blackness swirls in front of me. I had too many tequila shots.

"I've been trying to convince myself not to kill you for looking so angelic. I hate all things associated with Heaven and its occupants." He rasps.

"Kill me?"

His hands land at the foot of my bed and he begins to crawl up my body. His face looks menacing and I try to make my body move, but the combination of fear and liquor is making that impossible.

I notice two things right away, one, he has only

a pair of boxers on and his gorgeous, bronzed skin shimmers, two, he has a switchblade in his hand.

Why the fuck does he have a knife in his hand?

I shimmy away from him and pull myself up against the headboard but he just keeps coming until he's hovering over my body, his face in front of mine.

"I can see your neck pulsing rapidly with fear." He utters. "Why are you scared?"

"You just said you wanted to kill me." I whisper and then yelp when he yanks the covers off my body. I begin to shake with pure fear.

"If that's what I want to do, you can't stop it." I watch his full lips turn up into a cruel grin, showcasing his bright white teeth. "You belong to me."

I open my mouth to rebuke him but he begins to lightly scrape the blade up my left leg. I don't take this lightly given the fact he carved into my ass not too long ago. The scar is still angry and red.

He slides back down and his face brushes over my breasts then my stomach.

"I've always loved the power a sharpened blade holds," his breath is warm against my thigh. "It can lightly scrape the finest hair from the surface of the skin, or it can pierce the flesh and spill its secrets."

The knife continues its ascent and he flicks it against the strap of my underwear where my thigh meets my core.

"Raiden..." I trail off, fear stealing my thoughts.

He continues to push aside my underwear with that knife, slowly exposing me, and letting the blade's tip graze my pussy.

"I can smell how turned on you are." His voice deepens with arousal.

My body begins to tremble with want and fear, a tantalizing mix.

"You want me inside of you?" He asks and I mewl at his words.

Yes.

"Do you want my tongue to slip through your wet pussy?" I have never had anyone talk to me this way before. I've especially never had anyone hold a knife to my pussy either.

"Raiden," I tense as the cold metal presses closer. "I want those things, without the knife."

"But the knife makes it interesting and a little bit dangerous." He says that last word like he's starving and staring at an open buffet.

He reaches up and grabs my underwear, ripping it from my body. I suck in a breath, readying myself to scream when his large hand slaps down over my mouth.

"Shh, demon girl." He whispers as his face looms above mine. "We don't want to wake the house."

His hardness presses into my thigh and I arch my back trying to bring it closer to my core. I don't know what happens to my common sense whenever Raiden comes around but it's clear the bitch is nowhere to be found. This is a man that rips the clothes off my body and holds a knife to my pussy.

Nowhere to be fucking found.

"Have you ever tasted another person's blood before?" He whispers.

I can't answer with his hand over my mouth so I shake my head.

"It's nothing like when you taste your own." He dips his head and licks over the freshly healed cut on my neck. "Blood is like wine, it holds hints of flavors telling you about each person. Even Catholic churches tell you to drink the blood of Christ and eat his flesh, so it can't be wrong." He says sarcastically.

His words should be disarming but his voice somehow erases my fear and I gasp when I feel his touch at my opening. My muffled moan becomes a squeak when what I thought were his fingers is a hard object slowly being inserted inside me.

My hands land on his chest and I try to push him away, he's sticking the handle of his knife inside me. His hand comes off my mouth and he leans down, his lips just a breadth's width away from mine.

"Don't fight it," his eyes hold me in place. "Maybe I'll reward you with a taste of my blood."

"I don't need to taste your blood to know you, Raiden." I say to him and he stops pushing the fucking knife into me. "I heard your music tonight, everything you can't say, even things you don't sing, I can hear them in your voice and you have mountains of anger that reside in the deep valleys of your pain."

His head rears back a bit as he quickly covers up his shocked expression. The knife is removed from me and then the blade is suddenly piercing the skin on my inner thigh. His hand is back over my mouth just in time to catch my scream and his golden green eyes watch with rapture at my obvious discomfort.

His head dips and I feel his tongue lap at the running blood, then his mouth seals around the shallow puncture. He takes three quick swallows and comes back up to my face. His mouth is lined with my blood and my stomach rolls but my pussy clenches.

The hand comes off my mouth and I suck in a lungful of air. His mouth lowers closer to mine and instead of wanting to slap the shit out of him, I'm wanting his lips on mine. I want to taste my blood inside of his mouth, I want to know what we taste like mixed together and if that concoction is as addictive as I think it would be.

"You want to kiss me, demon?" He asks with that devilish smirk.

"You sound fucking insane, Raiden." I pant. "What the fuck is wrong with you?"

His eyes stay trained on my mouth and I watch as his twists up into a delicious grin. I want that mouth even though I shouldn't.

I lick my lips, hoping, anticipating he gives me exactly what I'm craving. He shoves himself up off the bed and tosses the knife beside my head.

"I don't kiss." He states and starts for the door.

"Why not?"

That's what I ask right now? Why not?

"Because it gives females hope for something they'll never have." He looks at me over his shoulder. "I can never keep them for long."

Then he's gone and I look down to my bleeding thigh, I'll be lucky to leave here with any blood left in my fucking body.

I grab the knife up from beside me and stare at the bolt of lightning, then I turn it to the other side and see a cyclone.

What is the cyclone for?

SING ME a Song

Sacrificial Lambs

TEMPEST

C.A. RENE

Chapter Thirteen

t's late afternoon by the time I roll out of bed. I would think last night was all a dream if I didn't see the bloody sheets and the cut on my leg. I guess that's how Raiden wanted to announce his arrival.

The girls are out on the beach, soaking up the sun, and having drinks. I don't see Deluge anywhere and the thought of drinking again has me gagging. I find Sky in the dining room and snort when I see she looks just as bad as I do.

"One down." She moans and grips her head.

"It's not so bad." I chide her and grab up some of the food laid out.

"Let's see how it goes tonight." She moans and lays her face against the cool wood tabletop.

"Let's avoid tequila tonight." I say as I shovel some chicken and rice into my mouth.

"Tequila is a gift from Satan." I hear a low grumble and turn quickly towards the voice.

It's the guy that was with Raiden the first night we… met. I know it, even though I've never seen his face until now, I can see it in the way he walks and his stature.

His skin color is a bit darker than Raiden's and his eyes are golden, but they have the same mouth. He also doesn't have the piercings in his nose and his hair is braided into cornrows.

"Torrent." He holds his hand out to me.

I drop my fork and slowly shake his hand. Then he leans over and does the same to Sky. She shakes his hand like it's a dirty wet rag and I snort at her again.

"Sky and Tempest, right?" He asks.

"In the flesh." Sky says around a mouthful of food.

"And blood." I mutter.

Torrent laughs and the sound does not match his looks. It's jolly and addictive, before I even realize it, I'm joining in. Even Sky is chuckling.

I get a glimpse at his tongue and gasp when I see the forks.

"You're the one with his tongue forked." I exclaim and he nods.

"Made in his image, right?" He winks at me.

I look at him confused and Sky huffs.

"Makes all the fucking sense," she chews audibly. "You're all Satan worshipers."

"Wrong." He shakes his head. "We worship no one but ourselves, there's no god telling us what we have to do to get into this 'Heaven' and we live what short lives we have here to the fullest."

I like what he's saying, I was never raised to be anything in particular, and what I did see of people that went to church were stiff, snobby individuals.

"Sounds really self-serving." Sky retorts.

"It should be." He grins at her. "Why serve others when no one is serving you?"

"Existential debates." The one named Squall comes into the room. "Sounds like the celebrations are truly beginning."

He's not as tall as Torrent and Raiden, but he's just as wide. He's built thick and where they are darker skinned with dark hair, he's pale with white hair. I can't decide if it's dyed or natural since his eyebrows are just as light. He has freckles dusting his cheeks and his mouth is curved into a cute, dimpled smile.

"Sky here thinks we are selfish men out to serve only ourselves." Torrent grins at her.

"And?" Squall asks.

His answer makes both me and Torrent laugh, even Sky has a ghost of a smile on her face.

Hail comes in next and he's shirtless with a pair of low-slung gray track pants on. I immediately zoom into the outline that's resting against his thigh. His thigh.

His skin is golden, like caramel, and decorated in so many tattoos. He's leaner than the others but he's toned and defined. He's sporting a long graying goatee and his face has age lines, but they make him look good.

His dark eyes land on Sky and the grin that forms is stunning. His teeth, like the others are a bright white and he has a ring in his lip. He's gorgeous.

"Hello, Sky." He croons.

"Hail." She has yet to even look at him.

If I hadn't had an instant attraction to Raiden, Hail would be my type, and he screams trouble which happens to be exactly my fucking type.

"I'm going down to the beach." Sky pushes back her chair. "Coming?" She asks me.

I think of all the girls down there with alcohol and my stomach rolls over.

"I'm gonna head up to my room and chill until this party starts." I rise as well.

The guys stay quiet and as Sky passes Hail he reaches out and brings one of her braids to his nose, breathing deeply. She swats his hand away and the guys all chuckle but I don't miss the dark look that flashes in his eyes. He didn't like that.

I reach my room and walk inside to a large man with a habit of cutting into my skin, lounging on my bed. He takes up most of the queen-sized bed and he looks at ease with his hands behind his head.

"Tonight, the dress code is leather, I left you something in your closet." He rasps and my pussy squeezes.

"Okay." My voice comes out breathy.

He finally turns to look at me and his eyes are the lightest golden green I've seen yet. They pop from his face where everything else looks dark and sinful.

"Come here." He demands and I am halfway there before I can even think about how desperate I look.

"There are rules tonight." He reaches out and grabs the hem of my shorts pulling me in closer to his side of the bed.

"What rules?" I ask as I remain standing and looking down at him.

"You do every single thing I tell you to do. Do not disobey me."

"I'm not your pet." I snarl and snatch my shorts out of his grip.

"No?" He leans up and snares his fist into the ends of my hair, pulling me roughly down to his level. "I own you and if I fucking tell you to fling your worthless self over a balcony railing, you'll fucking do it."

The pain in my scalp has nothing on the shock I feel at his words. He went from looking sexy to downright terrifying in seconds.

He lets me go and sits up. "Don't disobey, demon. Or I will fling you over a balcony myself."

Then he's off the bed and has his hand wrapped around my throat, pushing me to the double doors of my balcony. He swings the doors open and I struggle to remove his hand as he pushes me outside. The railing hits my back as he continues to push me until I'm bowed backwards and struggling to breathe.

"Am I understood?"

I can't speak and I can barely breathe but I give a small nod. I don't want to die and if it means I must obey a psychopath to stay alive then that's what I must do.

Thirty grand.

One week.

I can do this.

Sacrificial Lambs

RAIDEN

C.A. RENE

Chapter Fourteen

made a knife with an image depicting her name. She's the first person I've met outside of myself with a given name meaning storm. I was named Raiden and the other three decided they wanted names affiliated with a storm, too. And thus, the creation of Deluge.

"Everything is set up?" Squall asks. "They're really coming here?"

"They want to be witness to our greatest sacrifices yet." I nod.

We spent many years bending to the will of evil people, doing their bidding, and robbing innocent people of their lives. Our hands are saturated in the blood of the innocent and that weighs heavy on our conscience, no matter how dark our souls may be. Are we completely reformed? Do we repent for all those sins? Fuck no, we're still fucked up, we still crave the sight of blood, the sight of fear on someone's face, and we still worship ourselves.

We're just done with being used and ready to turn the fucking tables on those that decided to fuck with Deluge.

My demon is dancing on a platform with her friend Sky and the blood red leather outfit I gave her looks fucking sinful. Her jet-black hair is bone straight down her back and her makeup is smokey, but those lips are a matching shade to the outfit.

The top is a series of straps strategically placed to cover the bits I don't want others seeing but designed to look like she's wearing next to nothing. The skirt is composed of the same straps but hangs loose to mid-thigh and part when she moves her hips. She made the right choice by wearing underwear because I would've thrown her off that balcony otherwise.

She has yet to look at me and I smirk knowing she's pissed off. She's a little spitfire and I can't help but get hard at the thought of her snarky behavior. I haven't taken her yet because I like to chase my prey and the hunt is my favorite part.

Torrent is the first to get up out of his seat and he stalks towards the girl he chose. She looks like a snobby bitch and she reminds me of another that looked similarly. I wonder if they picked her for that reason, to cause torment inside of him, and once again bending us to their will.

He stops in front of her and she turns her back to him and begins to grind her ass into his cock. He lets her do it for all of ten seconds and then he has his fingers twisted into her blonde strands, wrenching a scream from her throat.

He begins to drag her over to our table and the girls slowly stop dancing to watch what's happening. He stops her right in front of the table and her wide eyes are staring at us with fear. I fucking love that look, it makes me feel godly. He shoves her face down against the wood top and bends over her to say something into her ear.

She nods weakly and a tear slips from one of her eyes. Squall stands, leaning over to her and swipes his thumb along the drop slowly falling across her nose. He pops it in his mouth and I watch as his eyes roll back with pleasure.

Torrent rises, keeping his fingers tightly fisted into her hair, and her face still pressed against the table. He looks around the room as he slowly undoes his belt and a few of the girls cover their mouths with their hands.

I'm sure they've heard the rumors about us and the debauchery we get up to, but witnessing it is a whole other story. And if after tonight they want to run, well like I said, the chase is my favorite part.

His belt falls apart and I can see the bulge at the front of his chinos, growing as he watches the girl cry. He yanks up her tiny leather skirt, rips her thong off her body, and tosses it to the center of the table.

My brothers are going to be uncontrollable tonight because they've been abstaining, and I start to feel sorry for this girl in front of us, the first to be used. It's going to be rough, but if she's smart, she'll take it and try to find her pleasure through the pain.

Torrent has his pants and boxers down and releases her hair to roll a condom over his dick. These are strippers after all. Then he's working his way inside her and she begins to cry, her nails clawing into the tabletop. I can only imagine she's feeling like being ripped open as he continues to shove himself in.

Squall stands and goes around the table to get a better view, his hand running along the hard front of his pants. I don't know how long he'll be patient for and I lean my forearms on the table in anticipation.

Torrent finally bottoms out inside of her and she's stiff, her cries tapering off. I reach forward and pat the top of her head, it's demeaning but it doesn't come close to being forced to take a monster cock in front of a crowd.

Torrent begins to pound into her, his hands

gripping the globes of her ass, and his neck flexing with his efforts to hold himself together.

Not tonight, brother.

I grin when the girl's cries turn into little moans and I look over to my demon. She's watching, her body completely still, and her eyes focused. Her friend has her arms crossed over her chest and her jaw clenched. Two completely different reactions, if I didn't know any better, I would think Tempest is enjoying this show, and I grin when I think of how she might feel nearer to the end of it.

Torrent finishes with a loud groan and I nod my approval. He lasted longer than I thought he would and I watch as Squall drops his pants, rolling the condom over his swollen cock. Torrent pulls out and steps back as Squall takes his place between her legs.

The girl's head lifts a bit to look behind her but Torrent shoves it back down to the table. She begins to softly cry again as Squall slams into her. He's there for one reason and one reason only, to find what he's deprived himself of this last week and he cares not for how the girl is feeling.

The punishing rhythm he's set is shaking the table and the girl begins to cry harder. Hail stands and leans over the table to watch her face as it projects pure pain. He looks back at me over his shoulder and grins, his teeth bright against his olive skin.

Hail isn't even looking at Squall and his fucking, his eyes are on the girl standing beside my demon, and I know she's his fucking weakness. By this week's end, he'll need to be rid of the attachment he feels for her because we can't have normal lives.

Squall lasts half the time of Torrent and I lean back in my seat with a laugh. He grins, his face finally at ease and flips me the finger. He pulls out of the girl and slaps her roughly on the ass.

Hail stands, his pants already down, and the condom wrapper ripping between his teeth.

"This is a fucking gang rape." Sky calls out.

Hail stands between the crying girl's legs and throws Sky a wink. He pulls the condom on and Sky watches him with her brow raised. It'll be fun when it's her turn.

The cries pick up against the table and I know Hail has begun his turn on the girl whose nails are breaking on the wooden surface. Torrent sits back down beside me and gulps back a few mouthfuls of vodka straight from the bottle.

"It's just as hot being on this side." He laughs.

He falls forward and swipes the hair back from her face. Her skin is red and her green eyes shine with her tears, and it's beautiful.

"Doesn't she really glow like diamonds?" Torrent breathes as he continues to smooth her hair back.

She lets out a scream as Hail rams himself inside and releases, his head thrown back.

"You're up, brother." Torrent slaps a hand on my shoulder.

He turns to her and pats her head like the good girl she's been.

"One more okay, my bright little Diamond?" He coos at her and I watch as her face falls.

Just one more, sure, but I would say I'm the worst one. I get up from my seat and circle the table. I hear the demon gasp and I'm ready to show her that I'm not her fucking man, I can't ever be her fucking man.

I get to the girl's ass and look down at her pussy.

It's probably seen better days but fuck, it's still beautiful.

I run my finger up through her folds and find she has some wetness, not a lot, and certainly not enough to take me.

Torrent tosses me a condom and I snatch it with my left hand as I'm undoing my pants with my right. I pull my cock out and tug on it, I'm the biggest between my brothers and I know this is not going to be pleasant for the girl in front of me.

I roll the condom over my nearly hard cock and smile at Torrent when I hear heels hitting the stone floor to my right.

"You're going to rape this girl, too?" My demon calls as she nears.

"Rape?" Torrent says aghast. "I asked her if she wanted it. She agreed! Look at her there, she's not fighting it."

"She's screaming and crying." She exclaims as she reaches my side.

"We're all a little over average," Torrent jokes and my brothers snicker.

"You are not..." she begins but I cut her off when my right hand grabs her throat and pulls her into my face.

"You've disobeyed me." I line myself up to the girl's entrance, I'm harder now, and getting harder as I think of my demon watching this up close.

I loosen my grip on her throat and lightly run my hand along the smooth column and behind to the nape of her neck. She visibly relaxes at my touch and I almost want to slap her for being so trusting, she should know to not trust a single soul. What makes her keep wanting to?

My fingers sink into the hair on the back of her head and my smile turns into a snarl as I shove her head down on top of the girl's lower back. Giving her the perfect view of what she tried to stop. No one stops me.

She struggles against my hold but I tighten my fist, knowing I'm pulling out strands of her long black hair, and she stills. I hear a commotion to my right and watch Hail intercept what I can imagine is her feisty friend coming to the rescue.

I use my left hand and guide myself back to the girl's entrance, as I feel them both tense. I inch myself in until I hit halfway and then I slam it all the way home. Torrent's choice screams and demon cringes, her hand finding the girl's head and stroking her hair.

"Her name is Diamond." Tempest's eyes lock onto mine. "She's barely twenty years old."

I begin to chuckle as my thrusts work into this Diamond's body and her screams turn into sobs.

"She was excited to be here," Demon's voice continues. "She loved your music."

"She's singing us a song now, isn't she?" Torrent chuckles.

Demon continues to watch without interest and I realize fucking Diamond isn't doing it for me. I'm softening and it pisses me off, I want to be inside this demon instead.

So, I imagine it's her I'm fucking, she's the one bent over this table, and it's her screams shattering the silence around us. I'm hard again and Diamond is once again sobbing at my cock's assault. But all I see are the storm gray eyes watching me with disgust and I feel my balls clench, readying to spill my load.

I pull out of Diamond, pull the condom off, and jack off onto Demon's face. Her eyes clench shut but her mouth opens in shock and I push the tip of my cock into it, groaning through the rest of my release.

My brothers are clapping and whistling but the girls standing around are becoming weary. Good, this was never a celebration for them. I pull out of Demon's mouth, release my hold on her head, and pat her cheek.

I can sense her shame rolling in waves and I absorb it like the sound of a good riff in a song.

SING ME a Song

Sacrificial Lambs

TEMPEST

C.A. RENE

Chapter Fifteen

feel a rag being thrown into my face and I wipe off the cum, spitting out the bit in my mouth.

"We're leaving!" I hear Sky yell and then Raiden's sinister chuckle.

"You can check out, but you can never leave."

"You can recite lyrics from your era all you want." I rip the rag off my face and glare at him.

"My era?" His voice is low as he steps into me.

I don't back down and pull out a smirk of my own, "isn't it?"

"Chair." Raiden snarls and one of the girls rushes over with one.

He sits in it and throws me an evil grin, "Tempest here doesn't do private dances at her club."

I cross my arms and watch him with my eyebrow raised. He nods towards the table with his band mates and then looks back at me.

"Someone turn on this song from my era." He snaps his fingers.

The slow melodic sound of Hotel California by The Eagles floats through the room and he leans back in his chair. A hand snags into my hair and my head is twisted back.

"You're going to give him a good birthday dance," Torrent's voice growls into my ear. "Then maybe you will survive this night."

I feel the cold touch of metal against my neck and tense, "make it good." He licks along my ear and I shiver at the wetness.

Without much choice, I saunter to Raiden and decide if it's embarrassment he's looking to get from me then he's about to be disappointed, I have been at lower points in my life, so I'll make this real good and just maybe he'll rethink the next step.

I unclip the waistband of this piece of shit skirt and let it and all its weird fringes hit the floor. I stand in front of him in this bandage top and a ridiculously small G-string. The beat picks up and the lyrics croon through the room. My body rolls as I let the rhythm take me and I begin to move in time with the music.

I'm a dancer before I'm a fucking stripper and I'm about to show him exactly what I can do. I lift my right leg slowly and grab the heel, bringing it straight up against my face. Then my left hand is skimming over my stomach and down inside my panties.

Raiden leans forward, his forearms resting on his knees and I can't help the flutters that invade my belly. I know it's wrong, this man just brutally fucked a girl that didn't want it, and here I am wet thinking about it. His fucking monster cock slamming into her as she cried from its girth. I want that girth in me.

I drop my leg and move between his legs, forcing him to sit up as I grip his knees. Then I twerk my ass up and down on his crotch, almost purring when I feel him get hard. I reach up to pull apart the clasps for my top when his rough hands grab my hips and turn me around to face him.

"Unless you want the same treatment as your little friend, I suggest you don't take anything else off." His eyes are dark and his fingers will leave behind bruises on my skin.

He rises, forcing me back and then bends, picking me up from my ass as my legs wind around his waist. He strides out of the ballroom area to the sounds of the guys whistling and heads straight upstairs to my room.

My heart is slamming against my ribcage with fear of what is going to happen but also with anticipation of what is going to happen.

He kicks open my door and my body is slammed against the wall, my head bouncing off the plaster. His hand wraps around my throat and he squeezes, yet another place his fingers will leave behind their mark.

"I have never wanted to kill anyone more in my entire life." He snarls against my mouth.

He steps back and drops me from his arms, watching as I sink to my knees. I cradle my throat in my hands and glare up at him.

"One would say that means you feel at least something for me." I retort, rubbing my neck.

"Or that's what the little unloved girl from the trailer park was taught." He begins to undo his pants.

"I am not sucking your dick." I shake my head. "I wouldn't put it anywhere near my mouth again, if I were you."

The back of his hand claps against my mouth and I feel the blood pool on my tongue.

"Does that mean I care, too?" He mocks me and flicks open his knife, holding it just under my eye. "Undo my pants."

I know this beast of a man wouldn't even hesitate to cut into my face and if I continue to bait him, I just might lose my life tonight. As much as I don't want to obey him and everything in me is fighting my actions, I'm not going to be his punching bag.

I undo his pants and begin to pull them down along with his boxers. I know he's big, I saw evidence of it earlier, but as the thing pops up and swings slightly in front of my face, I'm shocked at the sheer size. That just seems fucking unnatural.

His hand holding the knife rests against my throat and his other grips the hair on the crown of my head, forcing me forward.

"Hurry up, I need to get back to the celebration." He raises a brow at me. "Lots of other females to fuck."

I clench my jaw at his words and his hand tightens, as I feel the hairs being ripped out of my scalp.

Fuck it, I'm about to enjoy this as much as he will. I stick my tongue out and lick along the tip, making sure to pay extra attention to the ridge. I'm good at sucking dick, I did enough of it to survive and I'm not fucking ashamed. I've just never dealt with one quite this large.

I open my mouth and relax my jaw, slowly taking him into my mouth. Raiden though, has other ideas, and his frustration is evident as he rams his monster cock down my throat. Now, I like to boast I can take a good deep throat with minimal gagging but I'm not doing so well right now.

Not that he minds, the more I gag and constrict around him, the faster he plunges into my mouth. The tears flow down my cheeks and I'm sucking in air whenever I get the chance, which is not nearly often enough.

I feel the knife come back against my throat and press into the flesh as he pushes in as far as he can, cumming down my throat. The salty taste and slimy texture have me gagging once again and he chuckles as he yanks me up by my hair back to my feet.

His hand holding the knife comes towards my face and I hold my breath, waiting for his threat. Instead, his thumb swipes up my chin and pushes into my mouth, more of his cum assaults my tongue.

"You take every last drop of what I give you." He shoves me back to the wall and stabs the blade into the plaster, nicking my shoulder on the way.

I hiss at the sting and watch as his eyes latch onto the wound, the blood rolling down to my chest. He leans forward and presses his finger into it then up over the cut. He takes his blood-soaked finger and draws something on my cheek, giving it a little pat when he's done.

"Tempest Skeigh," his voice is softer. "Your blood looks good coating your skin."

I moan at the contact and gasp at his words. I don't know what is wrong with me and I'm confused about this odd attraction to a man old enough to be my father, and dark enough to rival the devil.

He steps away and pulls the blade out of the wall, slicing me again.

"Stay in your fucking room." Then he's out the door.

I hurry to my bathroom, flicking on the light, and growling when I see a triangle with an eye in the center. The exact symbol I saw connected to the Illuminati.

I want to check on Sky and as much as she bothers me, Diamond too. I just know that if I push the devil too far, my body will be pulp on the pavement under my balcony.

Sacrificial Lambs

TEMPEST

C.A. RENE

Chapter Sixteen

I'm afraid to leave my room.

I'm rarely this afraid but I can't stop my mind from racing with images of myself being murdered and disposed of by Raiden. It could also be that I have not touched a drug in almost three days and I'm having a hard time numbing the feelings.

I want to check on Sky, I want to make sure Diamond is okay, and I want to get the fuck off this island. The first two are doable but that third one isn't happening and it scares me to death. If I were to disappear here, I wouldn't have a single person to look for me and I can't help but feel my chest grow heavy with sorrow.

There's a soft rap on the room door and I suck in a breath. I don't move right away and I swear I can hear the banging of my heart around the room. The knob jingles and my heart flies up into my throat.

"Temp!" I hear a harsh whisper and nearly moan with relief.

I rush to the door and throw it open to see Sky's worried face. I grab her in my arms and drag her into the room.

"Are you okay?" She asks me as I smother her into my chest.

"Yes," I nod. "Are you okay?"

"Yeah." Her voice shakes a bit and I squeeze her tighter.

She pulls away and growls in frustration.

"We can't leave Temp."

"Why not?" I crinkle my brow.

"I told Hail last night that I was packing my shit and leaving this morning." She sucks in a breath and looks at me with watery eyes. "He laughed and said someone was watching my mother, waiting for the word. He took my passport."

"Fuck." I curse and begin to pace.

"You can leave Tempest."

"I could never leave you here alone." I shake my head. "I will have to wait this out with you."

"Diamond is downstairs frolicking with the girls like nothing happened last night, she was even flirting with Torrent and sitting on his lap." Sky exclaims.

"Is she stoned?" I ask incredulously. "And if she is, where can I get it?"

Sky snorts and then she finally lets herself relax.

"We're going to be okay, right Temp?" Her big brown eyes beg me to lie to her.

"We will be if we do what we're told." I nod.

It's after dinner and I'm lying on my bed, dreading what's to come tonight. I promised Sky we would be okay but I can't be sure that's the truth. This doesn't feel right and those four men are not sane.

They work on a different frequency and live for only themselves, not giving a shit what happens to others. They gang raped Diamond last night and I watched her today as she laughed and joked with the girls.

Either she's also trying her best to survive or she's a fucking nutcase, too.

The door bangs open and bounces off the wall behind it.

"Tonight, is silk." Raiden growls and throws an outfit on the bed.

I haven't seen him all day and couldn't help wondering where he was. His bandmates were around and when I asked Torrent if Raiden was joining us, he just chuckled.

"Where were you?" I blurt as he turns to leave. He stops and keeps his back to me.

"Ask me another question and I will cut your fucking head off." Then he storms out and slams the door.

Not sure why the fucker hates me so much, I have been putty in his hands since he first jammed his fingers up my pussy in that alleyway. I pick up the outfit with my thumb and forefinger and watch as it catches in the breeze from the balcony.

It's see-through and a rainbow of different color silks stitched together in a halter top dress. Fuck him, tonight I'm not wearing underwear.

My nipples harden against the very thin material that's attempting to cover them. I can feel his eyes on me as I dance and my whole body is reacting. My nipples are hardened peaks and my pussy is throbbing in beat to another dark sounding grunge rock song.

"Are you as nervous as me?" Sky asks as she works her hips. "What will happen tonight?"

"Just keep moving and don't look them in the eye." I advise and she snorts.

I wasn't fucking kidding. If they don't have any reason to interact with us, then we may just fly under the radar, and make it through unscathed.

"Demon." I spoke too fucking soon.

I turn to the sound of Raiden's voice as he lounges at the same table Diamond was defiled on. They have a few large bags of cocaine sitting in the center and lines cut onto the wood surface.

My body thrums with a want so strong to sink my head into a mound of it and sniff until I run out of lung space.

"Come sit with me." He rasps, like the purr of a lion before it strikes.

"Do it." Sky whispers. "Don't disobey him."

I step down from the platform we're on and walk over. As soon as I'm in front of him, his arm snags around my waist and he pulls me onto his lap.

"No underwear tonight." It's not a question because the answer is obvious.

"I didn't have anything silk." I shrug and he surprisingly laughs at my answer.

"Want some?" He points to the lines.

"Yes." I husk out, my need overtaking everything else.

"Have at it."

I lean forward and snort two lines into each nostril. The buzz is nearly instantaneous and I moan at the blissful numbness. Raiden adjusts me on his lap and I then notice his jean clad cock hard against my nearly bare ass.

"I hate how much I want you." He whispers

harshly into my ear. "Would you let me fuck you, right here? Where everyone can see?"

Would I?

I look around the table and see the other three guys laughing and grabbing onto girls, not really paying attention to us. The girls are either dancing in pairs or drinking and keeping their distance around the room.

I roll my hips and grind my ass into his cock.

I would.

He pulls my legs open, having them hang on either side of his, and runs his fingers against my wet pussy.

"This for me, Demon?"

"Yes." I moan and close my eyes.

He circles my clit and then two fingers slide inside me. He pumps into me and I begin to work my hips in a rhythm to match.

"You see them watching you?"

I open my eyes and see animalistic hunger all over the other's faces. Hail has his dick out in his hand and is pumping furiously, Torrent is watching intensely, and Squall has his eye on my bouncing tits.

"Fuck her, Raiden." Hail groans. "Then we want our turn."

My stomach flips and I immediately stop moving. I don't want to be the next Diamond.

"No." Raiden growls. "But you can taste her."

"What?" I squeal and try to get off his lap.

His fingers once again end up curled against my scalp and I yelp as he yanks my head back.

"Did you want them to fuck you instead?" He growls into my ear.

"No." I whisper.

He shoves me from his lap and I stumble into the

table and right myself.

"Get up on the table and spread your legs," he demands. "You're already naked anyways."

I sit up on the table and mash my bottom lip with my teeth, I must do this or else I will be the next Diamond getting gang raped. I lay back, my head resting on the bags of cocaine, and bend my legs at the knees, spreading them slowly.

I'm open, completely bare to everyone, and I'm shocked at the zing of anticipation that skates just under my skin. I don't usually like this, I'm not one to flash my pussy around, hence why I don't do private dances, but this feels so bad yet it's so good.

The guys all begin to stand when Raiden's deep, raspy voice hits my ears.

"Did you guys think you would get a taste before me?" There's something devious in those words, a hidden threat just rolling under the surface.

I squeeze my eyes shut when I feel him rising and coming around to stand at the bottom of my feet. I can't feel him, but I can sense his eyes on me, and my pussy clenches with need.

He leans over me, his big body wedging between my legs, and his mouth brushing my ear.

"You're wet, Demon." His breath heats the column of my throat. "Tell me, is that for my brothers?"

"And for you."

"You want them to suck on your pussy and lick through your wetness?" His words have me arching my back and rubbing against him.

"Yes." I breathe.

"Good girl." He grins and stands back up. "If you had lied, we'd be fucking your asshole."

I swallow thickly at his words and cringe at the thought of his cock ramming me back there.

He pulls my legs further apart and flips the silk skirt up around my waist. His large hands wrap around the inside of my thighs, forcing me to open wider, and spreading me for all to see.

"Her pussy is so fucking gorgeous." I hear Hail moan.

"Looks like it'll taste so good." Torrent adds.

Their words have me nearly screaming my arousal and I do scream out when Raiden's tongue licks a straight line from my asshole to my clit. He groans into my pebbled bundle of nerves and I grab onto his head, forcing him in closer.

He sucks my clit into his mouth while slapping my hands away, and bites down roughly. I'm screaming again as he roughly jams three fingers inside me and lashes his tongue against the sensitive nub. I'm shocked when I feel the orgasm rushing through me without preamble and my back completely leaves the table as I feel my fluid squirt against his face.

Never has that ever happened.

I've heard stories of girls squirting but I have never done it... until now. Raiden doesn't stop as he licks and slurps every bit and I'm once again climbing that crest while watching him.

He leans up and his whole face is glistening with my juices. Those golden green eyes watch me with an intensity that has my insides quaking and I reach for him, wanting to touch him.

He snaps his head back and nods to Hail. It's his turn. My stomach roils with apprehension as Hail gets between my legs and grins wickedly at me.

"I'm about to slurp every bit of this pinkness, girl." He groans and dips his head.

I'm sensitive after Raiden but my pussy is a greedy bitch and I feel myself growing wet and ready to come again. He's good, a little sloppy, and he was right about the slurping. Not as good as Raiden though, and when I look over at the fucker, he grins knowingly.

It takes a bit of time but Hail brings me to orgasm and I may have over exaggerated a bit. Raiden chuckles like he knows and I curl my fist as I think about using his sack as a punching bag.

"Squall." Raiden calls out.

Squall is pale and when his hands land on my thighs, the contrast is startling.

He doesn't say anything, just looks at my pussy, and licks his lips. His fingers run through my folds and I whimper when they make contact with my sensitive clit.

"You're only halfway there, little one." He grins at me.

Fuck.

He slips two fingers inside me and begins to pump, the sounds of my previous releases loud in my ears. I don't think I can come again, I'm starting to feel a bit sore, and my clit is so fucking sensitive it hurts. I don't voice it for fear of Raiden changing his mind and letting the guys fuck me in the ass. I can take this discomfort but I don't think I would live through a gang ass bang.

"She's so tight." Squall groans and slips a third finger in.

I whimper at the intrusion and he bends down, blowing air along my clit. It's actually soothing and when his tongue begins to feather against it, I can feel the beginnings of another orgasm simmering low in my belly.

I begin to grind on Squall's face as he removes his fingers and replaces them with his tongue. My fingers slip through his white-blonde hair and I begin to pant when his nose hits my clit.

I feel a hand smooth down my hair and I look to see Raiden watching me with admiration. He's enjoying watching his boys have their way with me and the look on his face has me toppling over the edge once more.

Squall stands and licks his lips loudly. "You taste like sunshine, little one."

That's new.

Torrent's big body steps up, casting a shadow across mine, and blocking all view. He leans forward, his hands landing on either side of my waist, and his face leans down over mine.

"That pussy has been devoured." I see the forks in his tongue as he speaks. "I'm an ass man myself."

"Ass...?" My heart thumps as he gets back up and flips me around.

I look at Raiden with panic and the fucker just winks at me. Torrent's hands begin to glide up the back of my thighs and he grabs my waist, propping me up onto my knees. He grabs both ass cheeks in his hands and spreads me open wide.

"Raiden..." I begin but I'm quickly cut off when I feel Torrent flick that tongue against my puckered hole.

No way. He is not actually going to eat my ass, is he?

His lips seal around my rear and he begins to suck and lick it. I guess he is. It's a different feeling, not unpleasant, and I know my self-consciousness is preventing it from being as good as it could be.

He slips one finger into my pussy and continues

to lash my asshole with his forked tongue. I let myself go and feel everything he's doing, my insides quivering. His mouth moves away and I feel a finger start to breach me. I don't want to stop him since I can feel myself on the brink of another release.

I push my ass back and he slides in further, eliciting a loud moan from me.

"That's right, sweetness." He croons. "You like your ass played with."

I do.

"She's so complicit and fucking tight." Torrent says and I hear Raiden hum his agreement.

Torrent adds another finger in my pussy and begins to increase his speed. I hang my head and begin to pant as shockingly my body begins to climb again. The coke is most definitely helping, otherwise I would be a pile of mush on the tabletop.

I begin to tighten around his fingers and he removes the one in my ass, opting to lick it instead. At the feel of his warm wet tongue, I crash so hard, my insides are clenching, and my juices drip to the tabletop.

"Mmm," Torrent withdraws from me. "Look at that."

I don't care what they're looking at, I fall to the table with a sigh, and my eyes close of their own volition.

I'm a fucking fan for ass play.

SING ME a Song

RAIDEN

C.A. RENE

Chapter Seventeen

She's out for the count, strewn across the table, and clutching a bag of cocaine to her chest like a pillow. Her skirt is still up around her waist and her pussy is dripping with satisfaction.

"She would've been accepted with highest regard." Hail mumbles and I nod my agreement.

She would've been and that's why they chose her. I pick her up gently in my arms and nod to Torrent to start the next part of the night, I'm glad she'll be asleep.

The sheep are the most relaxed if they don't notice the blade coming towards their throats.

"This is a week-long celebration for our group's leader." Torrent's voice hums over the mic. "Tonight, marks the beginning of our cleansing."

The girls begin to mumble and chat amongst themselves, a rippling effect going around the room in a wave. I am sitting in the center between Squall and Hail while Torrent continues to talk about the importance of giving back to the one that provides.

The double doors open and in walks Magister Markus. He's one of the top leaders for the New York group. Tonight, is his night to watch his pick for Squall and dance in the aftermath.

Torrent drops the mic and gives a brief nod to Squall, who rises out of his seat. He goes towards the lady he gave his knife to and drags her in for a long sensual kiss. She visibly relaxes in his arms and he slowly walks her back towards the stage. He releases her from his hold and smiles wide.

"Dance for us tonight, sweetheart?" He asks her, running his thumb along her bottom lip.

Hail gets up and begins to usher the other girls out of the room, telling them this is a private show, and to get some much-needed rest for tomorrow. A few protest, wanting to continue their drinking but he's quick to shoot them down and telling them to party in their own rooms.

"Tell us your name." He asks her.

"They call me Star..."

"No," Squall cuts her off. "Your real name."

"Shannon." She whispers.

I chance a look at Markus and watch as his attention is rapt on this Shannon he chose for our first night.

"Thank you for your time." Squall kisses her cheek and waves towards the small stage. "Please, if you will."

Shannon is a bigger girl, but her body is beautiful, and proportionately perfect. Her full hips swing in tune with the music and I begin to grow hard watching how she works her body. Her long black hair reminds me of my demon and now I'm rock hard, aching for release.

Her shirt comes off and is thrown to the side as she turns to face us, her hands inadequately holding her breasts' fullness. She gyrates her hips from left to right and I watch Squall bite his fist, the lust evident in his gaze. He stands up and walks to her, his arms outstretched.

"Can I dance with you, Shannon?" He asks. "Can I help you fly?"

Her brow crinkles in slight confusion but after a beat she nods her approval. That's all Markus needs, for them to agree to be our sacrifice, and to accept their fate.

Squall goes to stand behind her and grabs onto her hips, swinging with her softly. His left hand skims up her torso and over her gorgeous tits, stopping as he clenches it around her throat.

Markus walks to the front of the stage, staring up at them, and waiting for the spray of blood to coat his skin.

"Thank you for your sacrifice, Shannon." Markus says with an evil grin.

Squall quickly turns Shannon around to face him and I storm to Markus' back, the glint of my blade reflecting the light. Then I slam it through his back into the heart, his mouth opening in a silent scream.

"Thank you for your sacrifice, Markus." Squall says, his eyes closing.

"Thank you for your sacrifice, Markus." The rest of us repeat as he slumps to the ground.

Squall keeps Shannon's face buried into his chest and ushers her out the door. We will have her off the island and thirty grand richer, that NDA firm in keeping her mouth shut.

I pull the blade from Markus' heart and roll him onto his back, those dead unseeing eyes peering to the sky. We bow our heads and I imagine him burning in a never-ending inferno.

Squall is once again back at our sides as we breathe in the bliss of our cleansing.

"Come brothers," Squall claps his hands and

that wicked smile plays on his lips. "Let's celebrate his sacrifice for us and watch as all our dreams come true."

They all stand as I bury the blade into Markus' chest, cutting through the ribcage, and locating the heart underneath. My arms are coated in blood up to my elbows as I open his chest cavity and rip out his heart.

I lift it up over my head, letting the blood run down over my hair, and drip down my face. I pass the heart to Squall and watch as the wet warmth runs down his white hair, unto his face. He holds it up over his head, tipping his face back, and squeezing it until the blood flows over his chest. Then he passes it to Torrent.

"One down," I murmur. "Three more to go."

Let the games begin.

SING ME a Song

Sacrificial Lambs

TEMPEST

C.A. RENE

Chapter Eighteen

I open my eyes and the room is awash with the reds and golds of early morning light. I passed out hard last night after the guys had their feast of my pussy and my ass. I stretch my arms over my head and my hand connects with warm flesh. I look to my left in a panic and see Raiden sleeping soundly beside me, but that's not the alarming part.

His body is covered in blood.

I sit up and quickly run my hands over his chest, searching for a stab wound.

"It's not mine." His voice is low and gruff with sleep.

"What happened?" I gasp, my hands still pressed to his sticky chest.

He opens his eyes and looks up at me. "Are you worried about my wellbeing?"

"Raiden, this is a lot of blood." I lift my hands and see the sticky residue.

It looks like he haphazardly wiped it from his face, but his skin is still shaded with crimson, and his eyebrows have dried clumps in them.

He flips me over onto my back and hovers over my face. "I got to taste you last night and now I want to feel you."

My heart flips with his words and I gasp when I feel his cock bob against my thigh, he's completely naked.

I'm still in my dress from last night so there's no barrier keeping him from me and the thought has me growing wet.

"Where did the blood come from, Raiden?" I try to keep my mind coherent.

"Open for me, Demon." He growls and I do just that.

My legs fall open and his big hands slide under my ass, propping me up. The tip of his cock pushes against my entrance but he's met with resistance and I can already imagine what he's going to feel like. His grip on my ass tightens and he spreads me open further, pushing himself in harder. The burn is the first thing I feel as the large mushroom tip breaches me, then it's the feeling of being stretched to a point of damage, and when he slams himself in without any regard to my pain, I feel like he's just crushed my cervix.

"Fuck," he groans, his face in my neck. "You're so tight."

What he doesn't know is I've only done this two other times and never with anyone this large. Not that I didn't know what opening my legs to him would bring me, I did see him fuck Diamond, and I still wanted him.

I watch his face, pink with blood, and the blood caked on his chest breaking off, as he moves into my body.

"Did you kill another bird?" I ask as he stills inside me. "Like you do on stage?"

"Yeah, I did." His full lips pull back from his white teeth. "And it's soaring high in the sky."

He pulls out and slams back in, causing me to scream out painfully. It feels like he's ripping my insides as he lays into me and never once checks to see if my screams are indeed of pleasure. It takes a while but I begin to get used to his size and I feel myself getting wetter, pleasure slowly replacing the pain. My hands settle on his back and when he increases his thrusts, my nails scrape down to his ass as I scream his name.

"You need to come now, Demon." He grunts between his thrusts. "Or you won't come at all."

I want him to kiss me, I want that connection but when I lift my mouth near his, he brings a hand to cover it, and pushes me back to the bed. He has two more thrusts and then he pulls out, holding his cock over my belly. Thick white ropes of cum lace across the stomach and breasts of my dress as he groans through his release.

He really wasn't kidding about me needing to come. He pushes himself up and stands at the end of my bed, his muscular body covered in blood.

"Tonight, is lace." He points to an outfit sitting on a chair.

He turns his back and I see the marks my nails left behind down his back, scraping a path through the blood there. The door shuts behind him as I lift my hands seeing the blood caked underneath the nails.

What the fuck happened last night?

I walk into the dining area and the girls are sitting around the table quietly, completely different from yesterday. I take a seat beside Sky and look around at them.

"What's going on?" I lean in and whisper to Sky.

"One of the girls was sent home early this morning, she was caught looking through one of the guys' rooms."

She sips her coffee. "Probably looking for money."

"What?" I snort. "Is our payment not enough for her?"

"I guess not."

Something doesn't feel right and when I look around, I notice the girl that's missing is Squall's choice. The feeling only intensifies when I remember Raiden and his blood covered body in my bed early this morning.

What exactly is the punishment for theft around here?

SING ME a Song

Sacrificial Lambs

RAIDEN

C.A. RENE

Chapter Nineteen

She felt like the cleansing rain after a drought. It's fucking with my head because I can feel myself weakening and this must be my life's test. The one thing that will take me to my knees and I'll need to rip myself apart to let her go.

"Brother." Torrent's voice breaks the silence. "Talk to me."

"I fucked her."

"Is it my turn next?" He snickers and I have to breathe to control the wave of anger at his words. "Nevermind." He chuckles.

"Maybe she should just go home now." I grumble.

"I don't think you're done with her just yet." His face becomes serious. "Besides, Kenny would be more than suspicious."

I'm not done with her yet.

"Stick to the plan," he placates as he lights the joint in his hands. "It'll all make sense when it comes together."

"Hail is the same." I say quietly and Torrent snickers.

"Hail has been in love with that girl from the first moment he laid eyes on her."

"I'm not in love." I protest.

"I know, brother. But you are attached."

He's right, I am attached and the lesson in the end

will be worth the pain of the teaching.

The girls are rowdier tonight than usual.

They're having body shots and even the guys are participating, snorting coke off their tits. I just can't seem to find the energy to join in and Demon seems to be feeling the same. Sure, she's had a few shots and I saw her bump back a few lines, but she's subdued. I've seen her subtle glances my way and after this morning, she probably has a few questions. Not that she would get any answers.

After the contentment of our sacrifice last night, I just found myself standing in her room and watching her sleep. So, I gave in and laid with her.

This morning when we fucked, she tried to kiss me, and I almost gave in. I almost opened myself up and let her suck out my soul, like the demon she is. I won't slip again.

"You need to let loose," Hail says as he falls into the seat beside me.

"You love her." I nod towards the beautiful woman with the long braids.

"I don't know love, Raiden." He shakes his head. "But she has a grip on me and I can't shake it."

I nod because I know what he means and I know it all too well.

"That's why I need her to hate me." He mutters and I feel that, too.

Torrent has been keeping special attention to his chosen and she's lapping it up like he didn't let us all defile her a few nights ago. That man's charm works fucking wonders.

"It's nearing two." He says and I look to the clock on the wall.

It's time and showing just how punctual they are, Magister Camden walks into the room, his robe skimming the floor.

As if sensing it, Torrent's head comes up from Diamond's tits and looks over at us with a small nod. My heart picks up with anticipation and I turn to find Demon's eyes on me, watching me closely. They need to leave, especially her, she's beginning to piece it together, and I can't have this figured out by one of them.

"Get everyone out." I snap and Hail flies out of his seat, rushing to round up the girls.

Torrent inconspicuously pulls Diamond back behind the bar and pushes her against the counter, devouring her mouth. If the girls notice her staying behind, they don't say anything, all except the keen-eyed demon, and my blood pounds with the need to fuck her senseless, then watch her cry as I choke her.

Once Hail has everyone removed, we resume our seats at the table, with Magister Camden, and watch as Torrent and Diamond take a few shots. She finally looks up and sees us sitting there, everyone else having left.

"What's happening?" Her voice shakes.

I don't blame her, she was already sullied at our hands, and now to find herself alone with us, the thought must be terrifying.

"Nothing, baby." Torrent grins at us from the crook of her neck. "We thought we'd have a private party."

"Are you going to... like last time...?" She's frightened and I can't help the blood that rushes to my cock at the sound of it.

"No." Torrent kisses her neck. "Nothing like that, relax."

She relaxes at his words but her eyes keep flicking over to us as we sit here watching them.

"Come and sit with us," he takes her hand. "Tell my brothers about the recent tragedy your family has suffered."

They reach our table and Torrent pulls her down onto his lap.

"Oh," she clears her throat. "About my aunt?"

"The very same." Torrent winks at us. Interesting, I've been waiting to find out about this girl's connection and why Camden chose her for Torrent.

"Well," she adjusts herself in his lap and her eyes pop up to meet mine. "I had a great-aunt Sister Jane and a few weeks ago she died in a terrible accident."

What the fuck? I lean forward, my eyes intent on hers, and rub at the hair on my chin.

"From Loving Beginnings Orphanage?" Hail's voice is deadly low.

"Yes," she nods. "How did you know that?" She looks at Torrent over her shoulder.

"We actually grew up there," he answers her. "We knew your auntie real well."

"So well in fact," Squall interjects. "She made sure to be our sole disciplinarian."

Her face blanches and her body tenses.

"Remember that whip?" Hail asks me.

Do I ever.

"Wait," she looks at Torrent. "I barely knew her."

"Relax, we know that." Hail sits back. "Do you want to hang out with us?"

"Yes." She says quietly with a small nod.

"Do you want to fly for us?" Torrent asks her and she turns to look him in the eye.

His grin widens into a devastating smile and she smiles back.

"Okay."

"Thank you for your sacrifice, Diamond." Camden mutters.

"Let's purge our anger, brothers." Torrent says loudly as he swoops Diamond up and away from the table just as Hail sinks his blade into the side of Camden's neck, pulling it around the front, and to the other side.

Blood pours out and his head snaps back, almost completely severed from his body. Torrent comes back into the room, nodding that Diamond is safe, and being escorted to the plane.

"Thank you for your sacrifice, Camden." Torrent says as he picks up Camden and throws his body to the floor.

"Thank you for your sacrifice, Camden." We repeat and stand to circle his body.

I just want the blood of this vile human all over my skin.

Two down.

Sacrificial Lambs

TEMPEST

C.A. RENE

Chapter Twenty

He didn't come to my bed last night and I can say I don't care but that would be a lie, I'm disappointed. I wanted him inside me again and watching him during the party the night before didn't fucking help.

He has this authoritative aura about him and the more I watched him, the more I noticed just how sexy he is. Yes, he's much older, you can see it in his graying hair and lined features, but he looks good for his age.

His body is sculpted like a Greek god and I can honestly say I had only known men with dadbods at that age. Those piercings give him an edgy appeal but his golden green eyes are what make him look dangerous. They're always studying and cataloging everything around him.

I wanted to go have a chat with Sky this morning but when I got to her room she wasn't there and her bed looked made up or never slept in. I circled the grounds but couldn't find her anywhere. Now, I'm back in the corridor leading to our bedrooms when I notice her room door ajar.

Did I leave it open?

I quietly walk towards it, not wanting to alert whoever is in there, and causing a scene. As I get closer, I hear them.

"Where is she, Hail?" Sky's haughty voice reaches

me in the hallway.

"She had a family emergency back home. Her great-aunt or some shit died." Hail answers her.

What are they doing in there alone together? I feel like there's something I'm missing between those two.

"She hated her family." Sky retorts.

"Not how she put it, more like they misunderstood her." He chuckles.

Diamond left last night? My heart begins to pound in my chest and I lean against the wall. She stayed behind last night with them and now she's gone, similar to the girl the night before her. The night Raiden crawled in my bed covered in blood that wasn't his.

"Don't Hail." I hear Sky breathe and then I hear her subtle moan.

There it is. So, Sky hasn't been hating her time here too much if she's been hooking up with Hail. I hear the smack of lips and soft moans, I push off the wall and head back to my room. My stomach is tight with apprehension and I can't shake the feeling that something bad is happening.

I get to my room and pull back my newly made bed to slip under the covers. I don't feel like being social today, my head is heavy and nausea is rolling through me. What are my instincts trying to tell me?

I close my eyes on the sun's bright rays and Dominica's beautiful mountainous skyline, forcing myself to let it all go.

"Tonight, is fur." His voice slams through my peaceful slumber.

I open my eyes to the sun setting and huff in frustration.

"I'm not coming tonight, dock my pay." I say burying further into the covers.

"That's not in the agreement you signed." His voice is dark.

"I don't care. I'm not feeling well."

Suddenly, the covers are ripped from my body and his large one is looming over me.

"This isn't a choice, Demon. You will be there." His face is so close to mine.

His breath fans my cheeks and our eyes clash, I feel how dangerous he is but I want him. I don't move, I barely breathe, and I lay still, waiting for him to do something.

His eyes rove over my face and they land on my lips, staying there as he wets his own. He drops his torso against mine and I gasp at how hard he is pressing into my center. His eyes snap back up to mine and his mouth hovers even closer.

"What the fuck are you doing to me?" He asks on a groan and then crashes his mouth to mine.

My legs automatically wind around his waist and my arms link behind his head, bringing him in closer. Yeah, I look like a spider monkey but he's finally kissing me and nothing has ever felt this way before.

His kisses are just as dark as him and his soft lips are a contradiction to his hard kisses, as he plunges his tongue into my mouth. Our teeth knock together and I'm angling my head just to get infinitesimally closer. He tastes like every single thing that makes me weak and I can't be bothered to stop it.

While our mouths are still fused, our tongues battling, he pulls down my shorts, and slams himself inside of me. I break our kiss to scream in the most pleasurable pain I've experienced and whimper when I realize he isn't even all the way in.

"I want to hurt you for making me weak." He snarls as he grips my chin and pushes his hips forward, forcing me to take all of him.

The stretch feels like I'm ripping and I don't care because all I want is his mouth back on mine. I pull my chin out of his grasp and grab his face between my hands, forcing him down to me. He comes willingly and those lips are back on mine. The kiss is initially soft, like he's searching and savoring me.

Then he pulls out and slams back in, taking advantage of my open mouth to fucking swallow me whole. He's matching the plundering of my mouth in time with the painful thrusts of his cock, and even though it hurts, I can feel myself coiling.

Our mouths are still bonded and my arousal is dripping down to my asshole. Everything this man does is intense and I can already tell the orgasm he's giving me will be, too. Every time his balls slap against my ass, I can feel them stick to my fluids, and I am on the edge of combustion.

He feels me tighten and grunts into my mouth, not once letting my mouth go. His arm picks up my leg, holds it to his side, and picks up the speed of his thrusts, hitting me at just the right angle. Stars explode behind my eyes and the force of my orgasm has me jerking my head back, ripping my mouth from his.

I scream out his name as my pussy clamps around

him and he slams himself into me, groaning through his release too.

He's quick to pull out of me and stands at the end of the bed watching me, his dick glistening with what looks to be my come and blood mixed. At the sight, I begin to feel the discomfort between my legs and press them together.

His cock still looks hard as he runs his finger along its length, gathering my juices and blood, then sucks it into his mouth.

"You're bleeding like a virgin." He states around his finger.

"You're hung like a horse." I retort, pulling the covers back over me.

"Your outfit is there," he points at the chair. "No later than nine tonight."

Then I watch as he pulls on his basketball shorts and walks out of my room.

Sacrificial Lambs

TEMPEST

C.A. RENE

Chapter Twenty-One

I really don't want to be in this room, and I get anxious every time Hail steps close to Sky. This is the most attention he's paid her since we've been here and my instincts are screaming at me something's wrong.

She's soaking up the attention, something she hasn't done all week, and I want to slap her out of it. How long has she been riding his cock? What the fuck else have I been missing?

I watch as Torrent grabs one of the girls, lays her out on the table, and spreads her legs. He then sprinkles coke on her spread pussy and leans forward to sniff it off, licking off any residue. Squall stands up and does the same while the girl writhes on the table, her head tipped back and looking at Raiden. Only he's not watching her, no, his eyes have barely left mine all night.

We're all in a different animal print fur outfits tonight and it's looking like a fucking safari in here. I'm in a two-piece tube dress with cheetah fur and it's fucking atrocious. I don't fucking get these themed nights either, it's fucking weird.

"Demon." I shudder at his voice and turn slowly to look at him. "Come here."

I know I should stay away, he's dangerous, and he's the definition of toxic, but I want him. I walk to him slowly, watching the debauchery around me, and hoping

I'm not about to have coke spread on my pussy.

He pulls me down onto his lap, his chest to my back, and buries his face into my hair. His arms come around my waist and he holds me a little tighter. This is different and I'm not sure how to feel about it. He's never affectionate, he fucks me and leaves, and now he's acting like he's caught feelings.

Join the club asshole.

"I hate what you've turned me into." He whispers into my neck.

"What did I turn you into?"

"I want to kiss you," he groans, ignoring my question. "I want to be inside of you."

My pussy pulses at his words and I grind down into his lap. His mouth opens on my neck and his teeth nips at the skin. He turns me around to straddle him and I suddenly feel eyes on us.

"My brothers are watching." He murmurs as his mouth brushes over mine. "They look shocked. Want to play a game with me?"

"Yes." I lick my lips, my tongue brushing his mouth.

His fingers snap into my hair and yanks me to his mouth. It's an instant battle of tongues and teeth. I bite his lip and he bites mine to the point of drawing blood. I suck his tongue into my mouth and he bites down on mine. It's debased and primal, nothing else around us matters.

It's like a switch is flipped and all I need is him kissing me, grinding his cock up into me.

"Fuck me." I breathe when I pull away to catch my breath. "Fuck me right now."

His sinister grin has my thighs wet in anticipation and I thank whatever made him wear track pants tonight.

He pulls the waistband down and I whimper when his cock smacks against my stomach. So fucking big. I haven't taken him like this yet and the thought of working my way down his length is both terrifying and exhilarating.

His fingers find my center and he growls when he finds me without panties.

"Are you fucking kidding me?" He groans and grabs my chin. "How will I ever let you go, Demon?"

I want to tell him not to let me go but that would just be foolish. He's old enough to be my father and fucked up enough to make me fall in love.

He lifts me up and lowers me down his shaft. He's gentle almost, not ramming his way in, and I get to enjoy it as he stretches me open. He's bare inside me again and I'm about to question it when a voice sounds behind us.

"Holy fuck." Hail mutters.

"Ride me, Demon." He says before his mouth is on mine once more.

I get myself fully seated on his cock and begin to circle my hips. Grinding my clit into him and gasping over just how fucking big he is. He hits every single spot inside me, his cock hits my cervix, and each downward thrust is the sweetest pain I've ever felt.

Raiden flips the back of my skirt up, exposing my ass to the others, and digging his fingers into the globes, forcing me to speed up.

I hear Torrent curse and Hail is moaning, but I don't give a fuck. I'm on the cusp of what feels like the most profound orgasm I will ever have.

"Show them how creamy this pussy is," he says against my mouth. "And only for me."

His hand slaps against my ass and I jerk at the contact, my clit rubbing forcefully against his pelvis. My pussy clamps down on him and the both of us groan as my release comes over me.

My hair is brushed back from my face and I open my eyes to see Torrent gazing down at me.

"You come pretty, girl." His voice is soft.

Raiden tightens his hold on my hips and begins to thrust up into me with renewed vigor. I'm sensitive and it's slowly moving from pleasure to discomfort. He stands us both up and slams me down on the tabletop, my vision blackening at the impact.

I hear the metal slide of a blade and look up to see him running it along my skin. His thrusts still hard and deep as he grabs my top, slicing it open down the middle. My breasts are exposed and my torso on display as he continues his ministrations with the blade.

My legs are shaking with exhaustion and my pussy is sore from his brutal assault, but I let him continue. When I feel the sting of the blade, I gasp and look down my body. I watched in a stunned stupor as he carves into the skin just under my breasts.

It looks like a star from my view and when he's done, he runs his fingers through my blood, painting my skin further. It's like the sight of red has him losing control and he thrusts into me a few more times before screaming my name.

The room is quiet and Raiden pulls out of me, pulling his pants up. He has my blood on his hands and droplets on his lower stomach. I sit up and hiss at the stinging of the newest mark he's given me. I try to pull my shirt together to give me some semblance of decency but it's refusing to cooperate.

"Almost two, brother." Torrent says to Raiden, his eyes never straying from my carved skin.

"Get them all out." Raiden grounds out and yanks me off the table. "Go clean up."

He pushes me towards the door and I do a sweep of the room, looking for Sky. I find her wrapped around Hail, her arms around his neck and her legs around his waist, they don't look to be leaving. I get a familiar burn of acid up my throat as my heart slams in fear, she can't stay here.

"Sky!" I call out and Raiden turns abruptly grabbing me by the arm.

"Go and clean yourself up." His spit flies into my face and my eyes widen in fear.

He shoves me out of the room and closes the large double doors in my face. That's when I come face to face with a scary looking woman. She has a grey sallow face, her skin loose against her skull, and her teeth a dark yellow. She's grinning at me and staring at the blood flowing from my current wound. I hurry away from her and the look on her ugly face.

There's something wrong here and I don't think any girl leaves this place of their own free will. I rush to my room, throw my scraps of clothing on the floor, and rush into the bathroom. I grab the terry towel bathrobe and scream when I see my reflection in the mirror.

It's not a star carved into my skin, it's an upside-down pentagram and I know exactly what that means. This heavy metal band are actual devil worshipers and I would bet anything that each of their chosen girls are sacrifices for some ritual. Fuck, I hope I'm wrong but I won't take the risk with Sky.

I'm about to run out of the room when an object sitting on the bedside table catches my eye, I rush over to it, and hold it up, the cyclone etched on its side making complete sense.

RAIDEN

C.A. RENE

Chapter Twenty-Two

She knows.

I could see it in her eyes when she frantically searched for her friend. I close my eyes and lean back in my seat, waiting for Hail to get this started. I feel anxious like we have to do it quickly.

"This place is in utter chaos." Magistra Karen says with glee.

"Is this where you kill me?" Sky's words have my eyes flying open.

"What?" Hail chuckles.

"This is what happened with the previous two, your chosen." She has no fear on her face whatsoever, more like acceptance.

"I told you..."

"Do what you have to do." She cuts Hail off, "but know that Tempest is smart and she knows I would never leave without her."

Tempest is smart and I think she knew from the very first sacrifice but she feels the same thing I do when we come together.

"Why me?" She asks him quietly.

Hail stands behind her and drops his forehead to her shoulder. I can fucking hear his heartbreak from here.

"Because you stand for everything I used to believe in. You represent my inner hope and as long as you're alive, I will never fully ascend." Hail's voice sounds pained.

"That's why I chose you for him." Magistra Karen chuckles, "you are holding one of our soldiers captive."

I know exactly how Hail is feeling and come tomorrow night, I will be the fucking same. He whispers something in her ear and her eyes widen as he pulls out his knife. I close my eyes, waiting for the moment I get to sink my blade into Karen and the bliss that comes with each sacrifice, but then my ears are assaulted with an unnatural screeching.

"Get away from her, motherfucker!" My demon flies across the room with the very blade I had given her, the one I had hoped she would eventually turn on me.

Hail is slow to react, since he was also lost in our sacrificial moment, and my demon's blade sinks into his shoulder as he staggers back with a yell.

The rest of us jump to our feet as Hail stumbles to his knees and Tempest wraps her arms around Sky.

"How mad would Kenny be if we killed his pick for you, too?" Karen laughs and looks at me.

"I'm going to take her and we're leaving." Tempest's voice shakes with anger, "because let me tell you, as soon as you send us to your devil, I will make my way back to fuck you all up."

I don't take her threat lightly and I can see the others are shocked in their places, too. I can't help but look at her and feel pride, she's so fucking strong. It's just a damn shame she must watch us do something horrible.

"Tie them up." I tell Torrent and then to Squall, "send everyone else home."

Torrent grabs them both, even struggling, they can't get out of his grasp, and my demon is cursing me to hell. Little does she know we're all already living in it.

Karen's eyes are sealed to the girls and their distraught, she doesn't even see me or my blade before I plunge it through the side of her throat.

"Thank you for your sacrifice, Karen!" Torrent exclaims as the girls begin to scream.

Torrent drags them out of the room and Squall hurries off to clear out the house. I go to Hail and examine where the knife went in, there›s a lot of blood but I think she missed anything vital.

"Take it out." He pants.

I pull the blade from his shoulder then take off my shirt to tie around his arm.

"Get Squall to sew you up." I help him to his feet. "I'm going to go help Torrent."

"Take it easy on her," he sounds a bit hazy. "She's protective of who she loves and that's not a bad thing."

I sneer at him, my insides are brimming with fire, and my anger is ready to be unleashed. She fucked up our sacrifice and now she's more involved than I ever wanted.

I head to the door Torrent went through that leads to the basement. This is where all our equipment is and not a single soul is allowed down here save for the four of us and whomever we deem worthy of our justice.

The stairs are narrow and I wonder to myself how the hell Torrent managed to get them both down here on his own. I let the dank, wet smell of the cement walls seep into my nostrils and follow the yelling voices.

"Untie her you fucking asshole." My demon sounds pissed and I can't help how fast my cock swells at the sound.

I walk into the room and find Torrent tying up Sky with Tempest beating on his back. I wrap my arm around her neck and haul her back into me, making her watch as

Torrent takes her friend's bound hands and hangs them from the large hook descending from the ceiling.

"What are you doing to her?" She screams and I press my mouth to her ear.

"I have to punish you or else let go of everything my brothers and I have planned for years. No matter what I feel for you, I can't fuck this up."

She struggles against me, but I force her still as Torrent wraps her hands together and drags her to the other hook. I watch as he pulls her arms over her head and drops the rope down. She tries to struggle but it's her friend that tells her to stop.

"Temp, stop. It's no use."

"Don't say that Sky." She grinds through her teeth, "we'll get out of here and then we're going to kill each of them."

Her robe chooses that moment to come undone and I see the pentagram burning red against her skin, still dripping with blood. I don't know why I etched that into her but I must admit it looks like it belongs there. It was to mark her as mine in a moment of weakness and no matter where she goes, she'll be mine forever.

"Let them hang out for a bit." Torrent says with a snort. "I need to clean up Karen and get ready for Kenny. His plane just landed."

I nod and watch as he leaves the room, then I turn to her. My girl with the stormy eyes and a heart full of pain.

"You should've listened to me. Now, you have to pay the price of disobedience."

She doesn't answer me but her eyes flash with a hatred so raw and once again she's become my fucking mirror.

"That is why you were chosen for me." I point at her face. "You think you hide it so well, then put yourself on a stage, and pray people won't see it."

"Fuck you." She growls.

"You are exactly like me, Demon." I whisper in her ear. "And now you will belong to me forever." I touch the mark on her torso.

"You're so fucking delusional." Her eyes widen, "sacrificing me will just cause you more pain. I'm inside you now. The Illuminati are nothing but a group of deranged fuckers that pray to something that doesn't exist!"

"You don't know how right you are." I tell her.

Sacrificial Lambs

TEMPEST

C.A. RENE

Chapter Twenty-Three

y shoulders are screaming in pain and Sky is refusing to talk. She just hangs there and looks at the floor in utter defeat. This isn't like her and I'm suddenly hit with how hard she fought me about coming here.

"You knew." I say to her.

She just blinks at the sound of my voice but her eyes don't move from the dirty cement floor.

"You fought the whole way, at the club before the choosing, on the way here, and then now you've just given up." I try to kick at her with my foot. "You knew about all this."

"So what?" Her voice cracks. "We just saw them kill that woman up there."

"You knew they killed people!" I yell at her. "Why didn't you say anything?"

"Would you have believed me?" Finally, her eyes meet mine and they're red rimmed orbs of pain. "I tried to escape it once, I knew I wouldn't be able to again."

"How did you find out what they do here?" I ask her.

"Hail chose my aunt ten years ago and she never returned. I Googled them and I went to a reunion concert of theirs. I saw the pentagrams and the blood sacrifices on stage. Fucking devil worshipers."

Fuck.

We're dead.

I thought maybe I could get through to Raiden, maybe use our connection to make him see it's not worth killing us.

"Raiden is their leader." Sky continues. "His birthday is celebrated with a black mass. But the days leading up to it, they party and choose one person to sacrifice for their church. This year must be big since they're sacrificing four of us. It's like their ascension."

"Ascension sounds really Christian." I point out. "Wouldn't they want to descend…. to Hell?"

"No, not like ascending to heaven, but rising above the natural human needs and emotions, things that bind them to the earth. Then they can concentrate on procuring every success."

"Fucked up bullshit." I snarl.

"I'm worried about my mom," she drops her head again. "She was devastated after her sister and now I'm not going to return."

"Stop." I try to kick at her again. "We're getting out of here."

"Touching," Torrent is leaning against the doorway. "You two really are two of the stupidest broads."

"Fuck you. Where's Raiden? Why did he kill that woman?" I ask him a flurry of questions.

"Fuck you too, he's coming soon, and that woman was a part of the church Sky was telling you about." He ticks each answer off his fingers.

"You really are Illuminati and Satan worshipers." I mutter. "So why kill her?"

"Worshipers? No. We worship ourselves, but they showed us the way and now they'll die for it. They took just as much advantage of us as the Catholics did."

I don't bother to engage with him anymore, out of all the guys, he seems the most twisted. He gang banged his fucking chosen for fucksakes.

He looks down at my open robe and grins.

"He's marked you."

"What?" I roll my eyes and look at him.

"My brother," he points to my torso. "You're his for all eternity. Fuck, he actually did that. You're practically married."

"You are all fucked up!" I yell at him.

"Hey, it's true. We carve that symbol into each other when we join for eternity."

"Give me my knife then," I grit out. "I need to repay the favor, right?"

He looks at me for a split second and then barks out a laugh.

"I can see what has him so fucked up." He points at me. "If you survive, you might just save him from himself."

"Shut up, Tor." I hear his voice and when he enters the room, I know I should feel hatred or fear, but I don't, I feel a need so strong it's all consuming.

"Get us down, Raiden." I yell at him.

And then I watch as Kenny, their manager comes into the room with a wide smile on his face. The look has my body rushing cold and my throat ceasing in fear.

"In a bit," Raiden replies and opens a drawer to my left. "First I need to punish you for stabbing my brother and ruining our ceremony."

"Fuck." I drop my chin to my chest and admit defeat. He's not sane.

I hear the cracking of a whip and don't bother to look up. He said I was being punished and to be honest

I'd rather a whipping instead of a gang bang.

It's Sky's scream that has me tensing as my eyes fly to her. Raiden is standing behind her in a loose pair of track pants and raising the whip again.

"Stop!" I scream, "it was me! You should be punishing me!"

"I am." He says as the tails hit the open skin of her back.

Her body arches and she lets loose another gut-wrenching scream. Raiden doesn't blink, he just looks determined as he raises the whip again and cracks it along her back. Blood sprays and the tiny droplets splatter against my robe.

Kenny has his phone out and taking a video while watching in complete rapture at the torture being inflicted in front of him. I want to watch his throat being cut open next.

"Whip me instead!" I scream, "stop Raiden!"

He hits her another four times and drops the whip after the seventh hit. Sky is openly sobbing and I am crying right along with her. Blood is dripping off her back and onto the cement floor, the sound deafening to my ears.

"I hate you." I glare at Raiden.

"You don't." He looks at me and I sob when I see Sky's blood sprinkled over his skin. "But you should."

He stands in front of me and uses his knife to cut away the robe from my body. Maybe now it's my turn to feel the cutting edge of the tails on my back and for him to relish in my pain.

The robe drops to the ground and I'm hanging in front of him and Torrent in nothing but a nasty blood-soaked cheetah print skirt.

His finger pushes against the pentagram he sliced into my skin and he traces the lines as I grunt through the pain.

"I'm going to miss the way your blood sings to me." I watch as he pops his finger in his mouth. "Sing me a song, Demon."

He drops his pants and I see his cock standing proud with a drop of precum sitting on the tip. Kenny's phone is now pointing directly on me and his face is euphoric.

"I told you not to get too attached." Kenny sneers at me.

Raiden flips up my skirt and bares me completely.

"Brother," I hear the warning in Torrent's voice.

"Get over here and whip her while I pound her little pussy." Raiden growls and fear gathers throughout my stomach.

"No." I try to kick him away.

It's no use though because Raiden is large and so fucking strong. He grabs both of my legs and hoists them up around his waist. His hands grip my ass and pull me in against him.

I hear the crack of the whip and tense just as Raiden lines himself up. I'm not wet at all, nothing about this is turning me on, and I'm fairly sure Sky has passed out from the pain beside me.

"Raiden…" I begin to squirm as he pushes himself inside me. "I know you sold them your soul, but that's not true. I can see it, I can feel it. Don't do this."

"I didn't sell my soul," he looks into my eyes, "I just promised to deliver other souls instead."

The stretch is too much and the burn spreads up to my asshole. The whip cracks and this time I feel the kiss of the tail on my upper back. I'm shocked and then all at once the pain registers and Raiden has himself forced inside of me. The pain in both my pussy and my back radiates at the same time, making me suck in a breath to scream.

"That's it, sing for me." Raiden whispers into my ear.

Raiden pulls back out only to shove himself back in and the pain is excruciating, then the clap of those metal edged tails again. I can feel my blood dripping down my back and the stickiness of it on my thighs.

My throat scorches with the efforts of my screams and I try with all my strength to twist away from him.

"You should've done as you were told." Raiden growls loudly as he thrusts again, "you should've just let everything be. You shouldn't have turned your knife on a follower of the dark one."

I want to continue to scream at him, call him a murderer, and bite his nose off, but I have no energy to fight and my voice is almost gone. Every ounce of vitality I have left in my body is focused on my staying conscious and I keep telling myself I will eventually kill this asshole.

The whip hits my back again and I drop my head to sob, my shitty life has brought me to this point. I lived in a hovel growing up, every dream I had was crushed by a sick father who never actually gave a shit about me, and now I'm here being whipped and raped the night before I'm supposed to die.

"Four more, my demon." He says in my ear.

Seven whips.

Three sevens on my ass.

I try to disassociate from the pain and what is happening to my body but every time that whip snaps,

I crash right back into the agony. He's splitting me apart from the inside while his brother breaks me apart on the outside.

Two more hits.

I can feel the blood flowing freely down my back now and I want to moan in relief when Raiden pulls out of me. His cock is red with my blood and I choke on a sob.

The whip digs into my back again and I fight the black that's closing in, I won't pass out.

"She's tough." Torrent breathes like he's in awe. Fucking cunt.

"She is." Raiden answers. "One more, Demon." He says to me.

"You better pray you kill me first, Raiden." I lift my head, my snot flowing over my chin, and my tears salty in my mouth. "Because I will kill you the first chance I get."

Kenny laughs loudly at my words and continues filming our torture.

Raiden's eyes widen a fraction as I hear that crack and my back ignites with the torture. I can't fight the blackness this time and let myself succumb to the bliss of the pain-free numbness.

Sacrificial Lambs

TEMPEST

C.A. RENE

Chapter Twenty-Four

"I'm so sorry." I hear a deep voice breaking through my unconscious bliss.

I groan as pain floods me from all over, my shoulders, my back, and between my legs.

"I didn't want this," a male sobs, "I would've never hurt you."

I crack open an eye and see Hail cradling a despondent Sky in his arms.

"No." My voice is hoarse from screaming and my throat is dry with thirst. "Don't touch her."

Hail looks up at me through his red swollen eyes and I wince at the pure agony there.

"I won't hurt her." He shakes his head. "I'm going to get you two out of here."

He sets her down and I exhale with relief when I hear her moan. He's going to get us out of here? What the fuck does he mean by that? He comes to stand in front of me and I bare my teeth at him, hissing when his hands land on my hips.

"You killed her aunt." I bare my teeth.

"I did, there was no choice." He doesn't bother to deny it. "That's how I first saw Sky."

"You are all sick."

"He marked you," his fingers hover over the pentagram on my stomach, "you were sent to save him."

I try to twist away from the heat of his body but

the searing pain in my shoulders makes me pause and whimper.

"I know." He whispers, "I'm just going to lift you down, okay?"

Finally, I nod and his hands land back on my hips. The second my bound hands come away from the hook, they fall against his shoulder, and I cry out from the blood rushing back through them.

"I grabbed you guys some clothes and your passports, but that was all I could get. You have five minutes to pull yourselves together and follow me out of here." He opens a water bottle and pours some into each of our mouths. "Kenny is expecting to witness a double sacrifice in thirty minutes."

"Double sacrifice?" I croak out even though I know exactly what he means.

"We never were going to kill you girls, they were our targets, but you messed it up and I'm sorry they had to do this to you both, there just was no other way. There are bigger players in all of this." Hail continues and I still don't have a fucking clue what he's talking about. "Kenny needs to believe you escaped."

"Where's Kenny's phone?" I snarl. "He has a video of what happened to us and I want it."

"That video was taken to appease the elders. I need you to understand, we are taking down an organization one dark parish at a time. It was necessary that Kenny sent that video."

"There's no way he'll believe we escaped, not in our conditions." I tell him.

"He'll have no choice." He shrugs.

Sky hasn't said much and she has yet to look at me, does she blame me? Hail begins to help her get dressed and she cries out when her t-shirt rolls down over her back. Yeah, I'm not looking forward to that.

I try to stand but end up stumbling against the wall and my back scrapes against the cinder blocks. I grind my teeth through the pain and stagger back to where Hail is helping Sky to stand.

"You have to leave now." He's looking at me but his arms are around Sky. "Can you walk?"

"Yes." I hold back a cry when I pull a shirt over my head. "Where's Raiden?"

I can run out of here if it means we don't die, but I need to see him first, and I need to watch as life leaves his eyes. I pull off the bloodied skirt and it lands just under the hook I was hanging from. I pull on my pants, almost heaving from the pain between my legs, and steady myself on the wall.

"I would pray that you never see him again, not until the next life." He looks pointedly at the carving under my shirt, "there's food on the plane." Hail grabs my hand. "You need to leave now."

He pulls us along and I notice a bag hanging from his shoulder, right beside a bandage. I smile to myself knowing I inflicted some damage at least and I can hold on to that for the rest of my life.

The stairs are the worst part and the pain radiating from between my thighs screams as I take one step at a time. Sky is hanging from Hail's other arm and I pray she will be able to move on her own because I don't think I can support her, too.

Hail leads us out a back door and I see a blacked-out sedan idling there.

"Can you take her to the car?" He asks and begins to hand Sky over.

I grunt as I take her weight and she moans into my neck. Fuck, she's small but the bitch is dense. A man jumps out of the driver's side and opens the back door.

"Get them to the airstrip quickly." Hail barks at him, his tone completely changing.

He kisses Sky's forehead and I envision myself breaking his fucking nose, he's lucky my arms are filled with my friend. I practically drag her to the car and when we both fall in, I can feel the blood dripping down my back again. The driver runs to Hail and then comes back with the bag that was on his shoulder. Inside are our passports and some more clothing.

"Do not return home, he'll find you." He calls out just as the driver closes the door.

I dig past the clothes and feel the stacks of bills. There's enough here to start a new life. I look at Sky and find her already passed out again, her breathing shallow and fast.

We get to the plane and the driver carries Sky up the narrow stairs, disappearing inside. I take the trek slower, the pain almost proving to be too much, and when I finally get inside, the driver is coming out of a room.

"Where is she?" I demand.

"She's on a bed in there," he points behind him. "She needs rest to heal. So do you."

"I want to go home." I whimper, wherever that is.

"There's some pain killers and water there. We'll leave shortly." He points to a small bar and then exits the plane.

I want to leave too, I want to get as far from this place as possible, but I know I need this plane to do it. I drop the bag of money and clothes then head over to the bar. There are some pills and bottles of water. I don't know what the pills are but at this point I don't care, I need something.

I swallow down two and ease myself down into a seat, resting my head against the back. Just as I start to drift off, I feel a hand on my shoulder, and the rumble of the engine starting. I open my eyes and stare into a set of deep brown ones, filled with pity.

"Where are we taking you?" it's the driver from earlier, his voice is careful and tentative.

"I don't know," I sit up and look behind me to the door where Sky is, "we can't go home."

"No, I imagine not." He murmurs, "you should pick a place well populated."

"You've done this before?"

"Only one other time." He nods. "Las Vegas sounds good, no?"

"Okay." My voice cracks, "Las Vegas."

I get up out of my seat and he watches me as I move towards the door I saw him take Sky. I step into the room and find her lying stomach down on the bed, the back of her shirt saturated in blood. I do the same, laying on my stomach beside her, and try to close my eyes. Her head turns and she looks at me, her gaze lit with fire, and her pain burning bright. She lifts her hand and runs it down my head, smoothing my hair as she goes.

"It'll be okay." Her voice is hoarse.

"How does Vegas sound?" I ask her.

"Sounds like we'd have no trouble finding jobs."

I chuckle softly and wince when my t-shirt drags with the motion. It would be easy to find jobs in Vegas as strippers and with the money we were given, it'll be even easier to start over. I don't know why, if it's something sick and twisted inside of me that has me thinking this but, do I want to start over? I know Raiden is sick, his beliefs and his lifestyle are twisted and unorthodox. That doesn't discount how my body felt in his presence, how my very blood pumped for him, and it doesn't explain why my heart feels broken.

Maybe I'm sick too.

Because no matter how I feel and no matter how broken-hearted I am, it won't stop me from killing him if I ever see him again.

SING ME a Song

TEMPEST

C.A. RENE

Epilogue

The vibe in here tonight feels thick with sexual tension. Men seem to be a bit hungrier than usual and my skin tingles with perspiration as I move my body. Ordinary Life by The Weeknd is blaring through the speakers as I begin to wrap up my set.

The men like me here because I'm known as the witchy one. The pentagram scar on my torso is stark white against my tanned skin and my back holds a story of pain and torture. I'm not ashamed of either and have no problem stripping down to show them off. I survived something horrendous and it's my right to display it.

"That's our boss lady, Tempest Skeigh!" The MC booms as I slink backstage.

I haven't changed my name nor my appearance and I made sure to pick a popular hotspot here in Vegas. I'm not a victim nor will I ever be again, I'm stronger than I've ever been, and I crave revenge.

"How was it?" Sky asks as I enter our dressing room.

"Boring." I huff as I pull out my vial of coke.

"You need to quit that shit." She tuts.

Sky no longer strips and she's become the manager of The Sanctuary. That's right, I even named my club similar to The Temple back home. I want him to find me but it's been nearly a year without any sign of them. Nothing in the news and nothing here, it's almost disappointing. Sky healed well and pushed forward, she handled her trauma with professional help and I am so proud of her. She helped me with my process of healing too and I wouldn't be where I am now if I didn't have her.

But that's where the similarities end. Sky has forgiven them and she just wants to live the rest of her life in peace. I respect that. Just like she respects that I will gut that fucker on sight if he ever shows his face again, no matter how much my soul yearns for him.

I drop the vial back in the drawer and grab the small metal item beside it, my finger brushing over the etchings like always. I was shocked when I dumped the bag Hail gave us and the knife fell out. The last I knew, it was buried deep in his shoulder, and I can't see Hail wanting to give it back to me. I've always wondered who packed our bag.

"You good?" Sky asks and I slam the drawer shut, the knife rattling on the inside sounding loud in our small room.

"Of course," I smile at her through the mirror on my vanity.

"You should go home and rest, you've had a long day." She says as she walks to the door, heading to her office.

Our 'home' is right here, on the second floor, and the doorway that leads to the stairs is in this very room. That's right, I live and work here, and I barely leave. I don't want to take the chance that I'll miss him if he ever shows up.

I know, it's sick like I said but I am obsessed.

RAIDEN

I watch her ass swing from side to side as she leaves the stage, her back a myriad of scars crisscrossing together. Their beauty makes me proud. I've been watching her for a few weeks, she was easy to find as I'm sure she knows, and as soon as the plane landed, I was here in her club. She hasn't changed a single thing about herself and I grin knowing my demon wanted me to find her.

The lights drop and the music for in between sets starts, the chatter of men rising up with it. She bought a place that looks eerily similar to The Temple and she even named it as though they are sisters. The Sanctuary. Not only is it a bright blinking beacon, but it screams Christianity and everything I hate. I have to hand it to her, she's fucking cunning, and her jabs are hits to kill.

I watch the next dancer on the stage, her face void of emotion, and her body stiff, this is a necessity not a desire. I respect that but she has nothing on my demon. When her time is up, she exits through the same door as Tempest, and again I fight the urge to follow.

"The usual?"

I give a quick nod, not bothering to take my eyes off the stage, and I wait for the next dancer. None of them hold her appeal, her haunting grey eyes suck you in, and when her dark, tortured soul traps you, there's nowhere to run. She was made for me.

I hear the clink of the glass as it hits the wooden tabletop, my usual - soda water.

"He's been asking about you." I say as I pick up

the glass and take a drink.

"She plays with her knife and dreams about killing you." She retorts.

I snort and finally take my eyes off the dancer on the stage. I look deep into Sky's chocolate browns and grin, her face annoyed at my mentioning Hail.

"What will she do when she finds out you've known about me all along?" I take another sip.

"Probably kill me, too." She turns and then calls over her shoulder, "she's done for the night but she'll be back on again tomorrow, same time."

I lay a crisp one-hundred-dollar bill on the table and stand from my seat, my eyes straining to the back doorway just beyond the stage. I want to march back there, grab my woman, and throw her over my shoulder, even if it means her knife will end up embedded in my back.

Soon, Demon, I'll have you singing for me again. Soon.

Acknowledgements

First and foremost, thank you, the readers! You make all the author's dreams come true. Thank you for taking a chance and reading my passion. I appreciate you.

Thank you to my family who just lets me be a hermit in my cave and write all day. I love you.

Thank you to my Alpha readers Jocelyn and Tash. Your honesty is so appreciated and your friendships even more so, I love you.

To my betas, Amber and Gemma, thank you both for your laser eyes and honest critiques. I love you to bits.

Samantha!! Thank you for your honesty, for how much you care about my work, and just for being you. I am beyond lucky our paths crossed. I love you.

Thank you to TalkNerdyPR for all the hard work you guys put into marketing all my babies.

About the Author

C.A. Rene is married (but dreams of a RH of her own) with two kids (assholes) and lives in beautiful (cold most of the year) Toronto, Canada. To escape from life's pressures (more assholes) she brings fingers to keyboard and taps out her imagination. Most of the stories floating in her head contain blood, angst, and dark, dark, love.

Lover of all things dark. I love to read it, write it, own it, eat it, whatever it. My addictions include Coffee, books, and WINE, in that order.

Join my Reader's Group, C.A.'s Renegades, for more Book News!

Stay Connected

WEBSITE
www.carenebooks.com

FACEBOOK GROUP
http://talknerdypr.com/RENEGADES

GOODREADS
http://talknerdypr.com/CAGR

BOOKBUB
https://talknerdypr.com/CAReneBB

AMAZON
http://talknerdypr.com/CAAZ

Also by C.A. Rene

Printed in Australia
AUHW020839010222
358998AU00001B/1